BEHIND
THE
BARBED WIRE FENCE

JENNIE LINNANE

Behind the Barbed Wire Fence
Copyright © 2023 by Jennie Linnane

This is a work of fiction. Any similarity to any person, living or dead, is purely coincidental.

All rights reserved. No part of this publication may be reproduced, distributed, or transmitted in any form or by any means, including photocopying, recording, or other electronic or mechanical methods, without the prior written permission of the author, except in the case of brief quotations embodied in critical reviews and certain other non-commercial uses permitted by copyright law.

Special thanks to my son John Linnane for the Cover inspiration and Miz Campbell for my Photo.

Tellwell Talent
www.tellwell.ca

ISBN
978-1-998190-39-3 (Paperback)

"Loneliness and the feeling of
being uncared for and unwanted
are the greatest poverty."
Mother Teresa of Calcutta

Also, by Jennie Linnane:

The Ironbark Hill Saga
Ironbark Hill
Irma's Daughters (*Ironbark Hill* sequel)
Joey: The Man from Ironbark Hill
More Heavens Than One
River Kids: Growing up after WWII
Aussie Bush Yarns
Aussie Farm Kids

TABLE OF CONTENTS

Chapter 1 Lucy 1
Chapter 2 Eric 3
Chapter 3 Bennet's Farm 9
Chapter 4 The Mothers 17
Chapter 5 Discovery 23
Chapter 6 The Shack by the Sea 29
Chapter 7 The Accident 37
Chapter 8 The Barbed Wire Prison 41
Chapter 9 Escape Plan 49
Chapter 10 Trading the Furs 57
Chapter 11 Josef 67
Chapter 12 Cat 77
Chapter 13 Lessons 83
Chapter 14 The Stranger 91
Chapter 15 Sister Casima 99
Chapter 16 The Decision 111
Epilogue 119
About the Author 123

1

LUCY

1938 Somewhere between the coast and the hinterland of New South Wales.

Stuck in a wilderness prison, I grieved for my old world, a community of normal human beings where I was free to come and go, choose, and speak my thoughts. My primitive dwelling was a refuge with nature's beauty at every turn and the music of waves crashing or gently rippling over the beach. The sanctuary, with its back to the east winds, was a home for my precious journals. With this hobby to occupy me, I was as content as could be expected, living and writing in a shack at the height of the Great Depression before it was evident to all Australians that another world war was looming.

    Now all this relative comfort was gone. The man's fortification of high barbed wire fences seemed impenetrable, and I despaired of ever seeing my old shack home again. His eyes watched my every move, and his huge dogs shadowed me.

The trio of ghostly sentinels were ugly, smelly creatures and ghost white, made so by their strangely close fur, resembling white skin. Voracious eaters, their cavernous mouths slavered and drooled as they fed on the remains of the goats, rabbits, wallabies—anything that their master killed for food. He provided no receptacle, so they ate off the rough board floor.

I intensely feared those hounds and could hardly bear to see the disgusting manner in which they devoured the revolting food. The slopping, guzzling sound that assaulted my ears and brain was dreadful.

The ginger cat, which the man called 'Cat,' was also terrified of the dogs, and she frequently shunned the portion he tossed onto a rock under the pear tree. We were prisoners, Cat and I, and our only way of escape was by risking terrible injury climbing over the treacherous barbed wire fence.

2
ERIC

Eight months earlier

Let me return to the night I met Eric at the local Christmas Eve dance. Although he was seated a few yards distant, I learnt a little more with each glance casually cast at him. His height was average, and his build had a refined neatness. He shyly lifted his eyes under the blond-brown hair and smiled at me, and I began to feel a stir of interest but wondered why this seemingly pleasant young man wasn't already dancing. I saw myself as a typical wallflower—even my girlfriend-companion quickly abandoned me for a good-looking dancer, so it touched my heart when I perceived in Eric another sort of reject.

Partners danced past, the music thumped and jazzed, and presently Eric rose from the bench to sit beside me. After a few moments of hesitant conversation, I began to feel drawn by his shy friendliness, and when he led me to the floor, I found that he danced well. My performance didn't match Eric's standard, but he assured me that my feet were in perfect step with his. I secretly doubted the truth of this but appreciated his diplomacy.

After the dance, my new friend drove me back to my convent home. He parked his boss's borrowed farm truck at the arched gates and, after a few minutes of chatting, invited me to the following Saturday's dance. He was pleased with my enthusiastic consent, and as we said goodnight, his lips lightly touched my cheek. I felt elated; my first boyfriend seemed to be a true gentleman.

Upon my birth twenty-one years ago, Sister Casima claimed the right to be a mother to me, and I grew up loving her. An enthusiastic needleworker, she had made a pretty frock in readiness for that next dance outing and wished me a happy evening. However, on the following Saturday, when she met Eric, her disapproval was apparent for all to see.

There was a good reason for this. The dear, concerned nun had walked across the garden to the priests' presbytery earlier bearing fresh eggs and a cabbage—products of the convent's back yard. Sister had stayed to chat with elderly Father Kline and to enquire about Eric, known to the old priest by repute.

Later, after corroborating certain information she had discovered with Father's particulars, she disclosed that Eric had an 'unfortunate' reputation. Her brow under the wimple clouded with her disappointment for me, and she uttered censorious warnings against my developing too close an association with the young man.

'Don't place your good name in danger of becoming sullied,' Sister Casima advised. 'There has been some talk in Rivers Bend of his drinking and other troubles, Lulu, which may or may not be true. This little town has already added what it could to the rumours, and that's reason enough to end the friendship.'

'But he can't be what people claim about him!' I fiercely protested. 'I *don't* believe it!' And I felt a spasm of contemptuous impatience towards those relying on hearsay to decide who is acceptable. Within the populace on the rough side of town, there existed a mob mentality, people who had never spawned an independent thought but followed the loudest bleating like sheep. *Let tongues wag, come what may*, became my motto, and valiantly I rose to Eric's defence, secretly thrilled by my noble gesture. What a silly, romantic dreamer I was!

As I had expected, Father Kline, the respected shepherd of St Declan's, supported the nuns' collective concerns. He amply endorsed the validity of their anxiety over my association with Eric as each spoke their piece. But the nuns' advice came too late. I was besotted and stubbornly unhearing of any words that incurred disfavour upon my darling boyfriend. And so, with this head-in-the-sand attitude, I continued to go out with Eric every Saturday night.

To his credit, Eric proved a steady toiler, and I admired that attribute in him. Mr Bennet kept him on at the farm even when he gave notice to several others. At that stage, Eric usually worked with a tractor and plough, turning acre upon acre of brown earth and then harrowing the soil in readiness for the wheat. He also baled hay and was a skilled shearer.

At the end-of-summer dance in the small country town, we swayed together as a single entity to the tune of Cole

Porter's "You Do Something to Me." Under the influence of the evocative theme and the seductive sounds of the saxophone and clarinet wailing and moaning, Eric ardently professed his love. I was pliant as a pillow in his embrace, and as we slow-danced in the subdued lighting, the words 'Marry me, Lucy!' softly caressed my ear.

Returning to the convent, we were glowing with romantic excitement, effusively chatting about such themes as *life partners meant for each other* and *lots of kiddies,* allowing our beautiful notions to rest during moments of breathless kissing. But then Eric suddenly became animated as a vital thought broke the spell. He remembered that the farm's cook needed a kitchen hand and eagerly urged me to apply. After a day of pondering, I took up a pen and offered my services. The answering letter arrived a week later—I could start in two weeks.

This point of my story deserves a monument—like a gravestone inscribed with *Lucy's Folly*—to mark the sorriest mistake of my life. A week later, under a veil of secrecy, Eric and I travelled by train to Sydney and were married in the Registry Office of Births, Deaths, and Marriages. I had worn my best blue frock and matching netted hat, and we spent our first night of connubial ecstasy in a city hotel. On our return, I began moving my things into the workers' quarters, the longed-for love nest of Lucy and Eric Chadwick.

But the sky fell in! There, in the convent's usually tranquil lounge room, Sister Casima and visiting Father Kline animatedly expressed their astonishment that I had descended so far from grace. *Married!* In a Registry Office! 'Almost sacrilege!' The old priest sighed gustily, adding in sepulchral tones, 'And without God's blessing!' After several lateral head-sways, he lowered his grizzled eyebrows—unvoiced condemnation of the world's appalling moral state.

So convent-raised Lucy had married without the highly revered nuptials. Clearly, in some saddened eyes, Eric's and my Registry Office wedding didn't constitute a valid marriage; on that premise, it was tantamount to our living in sin! I didn't care, for I had never aspired to sainthood. Moreover, my stained soul didn't meet the criteria set by the Catholic church to qualify, even remotely. Well, it was done, and despite all the religious dogma, Eric and I had met the legal requirements and were, indeed, lawfully married.

Afterwards, fully aware of the atmosphere my leaving home engendered, I was affected by a bittersweet feeling portending a bout of weeping. I packed up my things in the convent room that had always been mine and, with nuns hovering, lugged the bulging bags out to the front veranda. There were arguments; there were tears; there was anguish. My "family" expounded many valid reasons to convince me to remain at home. However, it eventually became clear to them that Lucy Chadwick was entirely enraptured with her shy, soft-voiced man. Finally, the motherly nuns, and even Father Kline, relaxed their stance, sighed resignedly, and wished me well.

Shortly afterwards, as I transferred all my belongings to Eric's quarters, I felt I was home and reverently placed our wedding photograph on a shelf with his clock and my crucifix. Even the simple sight of my things in intimate proximity to his—toothbrushes in the same glass, towel next to his—imbued me with the sense that it represented the sweet meld of our entities, the real beginning of our future life of happiness.

Sadly, as the months passed, I began to see, ever so unwillingly, the error of that naïve belief. How utterly ingenuous I was then! I had been a vulnerable, love-sick girl; I had spurned the advice of sages and would pay the penalty.

Although at first my husband tenderly gave his love unalloyed with suspicion, gradually I became aware of his character's duality. He was irrationally possessive. Indeed, now that I was his, I learnt that Eric was not always the *gentle* man nor the gentleman I had believed him to be.

3
BENNET'S FARM

We had quarrelled again, and I knew Eric was now watching me; I had risked a peep at him as I walked resolutely towards the shed. Earlier that morning, he had *forbidden* me to take the old truck into town—red rag, indeed! However, I wanted to collect my writing effects from the newspaper office now that I was no longer employed there. Anyway, it wasn't *his* truck. The vehicle belonged to the farmer, Mr Bennet, at whose property my husband and I now worked. The old, rattle-trap Chevrolet was available to all the farm workers, the only requirement being that each person contribute petrol to the tank. That was fair enough.

The day yielded a caressing warmth; the sky was an Australian August blue, and the scent of wattle bloom hung in the air, so it wouldn't have been a trial to walk to *The Rivers Bend Weekly*, as I liked walking. However, that would take extra time, and the cook, needing bulky provisions, had requested that I drive the truck to the co-op for them. Eric stomped off, angered by my achieving a short period of liberty from him. I shrugged to pretend indifference to his mood and then prepared for the trip into town.

Bristling with defiance, I pulled myself up onto the running board of the battered old Chevy and sat comfortably in the driver's seat. I was determined to show Eric I didn't have a shred of regard for the ridiculous 'obey' command of marriage vows. Yes, I'd show him, all right!

But the motor wouldn't start! I looked across the paddock at Eric leaning on the cow bales wall and knew that he wouldn't venture over to help me. The fact that he remained oddly casual as he observed the situation threw a big hint into my head that, by some trickery, he had sabotaged the motor. Eric was like that, inclined to be vindictive when things didn't go his way. Indeed, this act of spite was very revealing, and the sudden change from 'married bliss' startling. Our rapport had fast deteriorated, and I realised there was something scarily wrong with Eric's mind.

Carefully ignoring him and trying to look unperturbed, I stepped down from the truck and lifted the tin bonnet as though I had performed the action every day. But what a display of complexity faced me! My rebellious spirit shrank. What did Lucy Chadwick know about motors? Nothing! I studied the greasy and dusty components and realised that not one facet of the engine was familiar to me.

Leaning over the motor, I recalled the farmworkers' recent casual mention during the tea break, which they called 'smoko,' of such terms as carburettor, distributor, gaskets, and other names equally mysterious to me. I wished I had taken better notice of their talk that day. Now my eyes stared in deep puzzlement, and a sinking sense of defeat made me want to cry with frustration. I knew Eric would be elated.

At that time, there was a prevailing misconception among some loftier-minded men that only they possessed the requisite strength and intellect to drive motor vehicles. Eric had already condescendingly explained to me (with the qualification, 'even though you're a woman') about the many potential maladies of motor vehicles. I realised that his warning had less to do with mechanical aberrations than his annoyance that I had found wings to lift me from the scope of his surveillance.

Nevertheless, an inherent faith in my gender's endowment of common sense came to the fore, and I drew on that now. It occurred to me that the strange, *octopus-like* thing shouldn't have been sitting there on the motor with its six hanging tentacles doing nothing. The weird component vaguely reminded me of the container that distributed milk through tubes to the poddy calves every morning. *Could this thing be a distributor, then?* I wondered.

A closer study of the various parts near the peculiar unit revealed six plug-type objects sticking up, lending themselves to capping. It seemed logical to unite the elements. So, carefully, my fingers fitted each lead over the head of each plug. That done, I brought down the bonnet lid with a clatter and made it secure.

Dusting my hands on a handkerchief, I risked a quick, askance look at Eric. He was still slouching against the tin wall, watching me, no doubt feeling an anticipatory thrill, confident that his superior mechanical knowledge would triumph over my female ignorance. Mentally crossing my fingers, I climbed into the Chevy again and reached for the starter button. Astonishingly, miraculously, the motor spluttered into life!

It was a moment of exultation for me, and I felt a brief impulse to leap from the truck and dance a victory jig for Eric's staring eyes, but fear of his reaction kept me seated. I steered the faded-red vehicle away from the homestead and bumped along the track towards the farm gate. Glancing back, I saw my enraged husband hurl a shovel across the cows' yard, effectively betraying his guilt. My euphoria vanished. I worried that he would vent his anger on the cows awaiting the morning's milking. However, I saw Mr Bennet approach the milking yard. The cows were safe now.

At midday, Eric and I returned to our workers' quarters 'home,' each from opposite directions and at the same awkward moment. He sat on the steps and, silently smouldering, yanked off his boots to remove grass seeds. I was careful to say nothing of the trip to town, much less to the co-op, and, determinedly maintaining my reserve, began sawing bread for sandwiches. We became excessively conscious of each other, of every sound, and even our slightest movement. My nerves were strung taut, ready to jump at the first sound from him. Even clearing my throat, the sound contrasting with the restrained atmosphere of the room, jarred as a rasping bark.

Strangely, Eric had always accredited me with a full measure of feminine docility, but a war of wills was at work here. I endured it all in cold reserve—indeed, I often bore this silent treatment as one bears a headache. My stubborn silence further inflamed him, and he finally broke the ice in monosyllabic mode. I felt satisfied that my nerves had withstood the strain without uttering a word under the tyrannical chill.

Eric effected a noisy business of dragging the chair out from the table, as if it had been glued to the floor. Then the interrogation began.

'Who taught *you* about motors?' he demanded.

'No one. I worked it out,' I said a little smugly.

'Huh! You think you're clever, don't you?'

I shrugged. 'Well, I'm not backward.'

'Hmph! See anyone you know in town?'

I sighed, exasperated. 'Only the editor.'

Eric chewed over that while he munched on his sandwich. 'Had a good whinge about me, did you, to your pervy old boss?' he asked sarcastically in as casual a tone as he could manage.

I offered no defence of my roving-eyed boss, for that would only prolong the prying. 'Oh, why would I, Eric? Credit me with a bit of decorum!' I shot back.

Eric stared hard at me, surprised by my bold riposte, then pulled down his mouth corners, presenting an ugly, menacing expression.

'Stop at the co-op, did you, to impress the boys with your driving skills—and curvy figure? Enjoy the whistles, did you? *Did you, Lucy?*' He shouted the last words as though I were deaf.

And so the absurdity continued. I shook my head to dispel the stupid hypotheses and assumptions as he fired them, and I endeavoured to swallow my food past the emotional lump rising. Eric's voice grew increasingly agitated. The intonation became thinner and soared higher as he worked himself up to a jealous crescendo—and I thought of Hitler. Only the time of the clock and the obligation to return to our respective duties saved me that awful day.

Eric's attitude bewildered me. No one regarded Lucy Chadwick as a flirtatious or an exhibitionist person, but Eric often attributed low motives to me, as though I were the town trollop. After collecting my things from the newspaper office, I had, indeed, driven into the expansive receiving yard of the co-op. Carefully, I'd backed the truck to the loading bay and alighted to place the cook's order in the hands of the waiting foreman.

I was not long there. Several workers naturally cast their eyes over the old vehicle with the uncommon sight of its woman driver, but only that interested them. I had no inflated opinion of my appeal and was modestly dressed. Moreover, the men who worked there were decent, hardworking husbands and fathers, so I found Eric's crazy accusations incredibly insulting to me and to the men he had maligned by implication.

Eric's outrage that I had thwarted his attempt to keep me grounded and that I had discerned his mischief and fixed the motor made my nerves quiver. That evening, out it came again. He could barely stand still, and the more his suspicious mind tortured him, the worse his language became. Indeed, the expletives bursting from his mouth were akin to a fuse advancing in sputtering increments towards dynamite. I knew he would explode and then strike me and afterwards sob and supplicate for my forgiveness. That was the pitiful pattern.

It may be superfluous to state that my love for Eric had long since withered and that I planned to leave him as soon as possible. Observing him afterwards, sulking over another bottle of beer, I found it difficult to remember a single aspect about him that initially had so attracted me. Even his blue eyes were like electric sparks to me now.

4

THE MOTHERS

The St Declan's Convent was the only home I had ever known. The charming, Federation-style house also was a refuge for several others who had been abandoned at birth and afterwards failed to qualify for adoption. They were the rejects, the outcasts, the unfortunate like me who were marred by some physical or intellectual disability.

Sister Casima had long ago instilled an interest in the craft of writing in young Lucy Smith. Upon my maturity, that occupation found its purpose in the office of *The Rivers Bend Weekly*. Time fell into the past, and I became hugely excited about my work. I covered weddings, christenings, funerals, school fetes, and sporting events with renewed zest. My preference for writing human-interest stories predominated, though, and became the most rewarding feature of my job.

Many people residing in the small town of Rivers Bend retained vivid memories of the Great War. Confident predictions were prevalent among the knowledgeable, older folks of a second world war approaching. The anxiety engendered by current, disturbing reports of Hitler and associates spawned abundant material suited for my work, and I seized upon it.

Increasingly, via radio broadcasts and newspapers, Australians learnt of Hitler's notoriously monocratic speeches imposed on the masses, propaganda shouted from a constantly gaping orifice with an intensity to burst a blood vessel. Eventually, people heard about Goebbels and Himmler and the appalling Nazi activities. The rumours, spreading with the efficacy of the Spanish flu, revealed that millions of Jewish people were being systematically exterminated.

The editor, warning some caution, approved those topical stories for printing. Evincing enthusiasm, the generous man assigned a regular column to me, provided I could prepare sufficient articles to maintain a backup ahead of the weekly publications. I was thrilled about this promotion, even though it was only moderate advancement in a country-town newspaper. However, Sister Casima perceived it as significant and a reward for all her years of tutoring me. I was fortunate that Sister taught English at the convent school and provided additional instruction.

To my dear mentor's delight, I also became absorbed in journal writing, and she urged me to begin a compilation of notes detailing my own life experiences for a future memoir. My records started with the primary information of which Sister Casima had first-hand knowledge—the grey dawn when I had breathed my first in the convent home for unwed mothers. This angel-nun revealed how she had assumed responsibility for my welfare when the person who had given birth to me fled from the convent, never to be found.

I have never felt the slightest inclination to blame my mother for leaving me there. She was a mere girl, a vulnerable sixteen-year-old, and the ghastly sight of a newborn with a gaping cleft palate would have frightened even the strongest of maternal hearts. No doubt the horror of that single encounter affixed itself to my mother's memory, there to torment her for the rest of her life. I have always felt heartily sorry that she suffered such penance and wished she could have seen the result of the successful operations.

The possibility occurred to me several times that my mother's family had disowned her. Society—myopic, sanctimonious, and often amnesiac—wielded a cruel whip to young women then, punishing them for the perceived shame engendered by their pregnant-out-of-wedlock circumstance. The stigma turned kin against kin, neighbour against neighbour. The young "offender" often bore the scars of emotional heartbreak and physical injury (for inevitably, some girls had been raped). Rarely did the blame lay its true mark upon the actual perpetrators, who were usually free to continue with impunity their irresponsible actions.

Thus, the obligation to provide me with a semblance of normality—physically, emotionally, and socially—fell to the compassionate nuns and doctors. I probably grew as an ugly little creature through infancy, but so pitiless a claim had never fallen from Sister Casima's gentle lips.

As if Providence protected me, and because cameras weren't the ubiquitous marvel of technology they later became, there were no early snapshots of me. The first smile I gave to a Kodak box camera was on the occasion of my First Holy Communion, by which time my surgically restored mouthparts had entirely healed. I am grateful that the after-years were exceptionally kind to my features, and apart from the faintly drawn-up scar of the hare-lip, I recovered well.

However, there remained one insurmountable difficulty—a speech impediment. Because of my tongue's inability to pronounce many words correctly, I have always spoken with a lisp. Ironically, *Lucy Ann Smith* was the challenging label my teenage mother, wishing for a daughter, had innocently chosen. Sister Casima provided that information with her account of the dramatic moment of my birth.

While a nurse was attending me, and before my mother's eyes had opened sufficiently to focus upon my shocking face, the question weakly breathed hopefully across her lips: 'Is it a girl?' In her exhausted state, she barely managed to convey the names she had chosen.

It has long been my wish to have a name that excluded sibilant consonants, unpronounceable by my clumsy tongue. However, Sister Casima overcame that difficulty by calling me Lulu, and my formative years were rendered less troubled because of that compassionate concession. However, it's curious to note that everyone else called me Lucy, as though a sensitive conspiracy existed to preserve the special bond between Sister Casima and little Lulu.

Naturally, curious hypotheses about my mother's identity and whereabouts often manifested over the years. I know only my brown-skinned, dark-haired mother's name, at least the one she gave to the home where she had stayed until after the birth. Ida Ann Smith was that name.

Perhaps the occasion will arise one day to meet the challenge of finding her. However, I know that the possibility of her refusal to respond will cloud that endeavour. Therefore, the sorrowing thought has often occurred: to be twice rejected by my mother would strike a severe blow.

5
DISCOVERY

Although technically over, the Great Depression continued stomping a harsh imprint upon many Australians. Countless people were now out of work. I too had become a casualty of this hardship when my delightful job ended. Soon afterwards, another staff member fell victim to the coming bad days. Our regretful boss promised to re-employ us when the economy improved, and no doubt that pledge might have eased the hardship of his unpleasant task of dismissing two reliable workers.

After the quasi-honeymoon at the farm had run its adoring course, Eric and I had settled into the routine phase, and the mood entirely changed between us. I discovered the full force of my husband's obsessive jealousy. It was shortly before the incident of the vandalised Chevy that Eric's other self began to surface.

He had noticed me at the clothesline talking to one of the farmhands. The man was guilty merely of pausing on his way to the water tank for a drink. That innocent momentary chat we shared—without my husband's sanction—simmered in Eric's head as he worked the tractor hard until lunchtime. Then I faced the interrogation.

'What were you and that bloke talking about?' he demanded after a sullen, resentful silence.

I shrugged and looked at him, surprised. 'Nothing much.'

'Must've been something; you were both laughing.'

'I—oh, the roothter had mounted a hen, but Johnno wath only telling me about the dingo raid, and I—'

'Johnno, eh? Friendly pet names now. Cosy!'

'Oh, Eric! Everyone callth him that!'

'*I* don't! His name is John.'

It was a stupid, nonsensical, and almost irrational conversation, if that term can do duty for interrogation. I drew in my breath and, with a low voice, said levelly to the ground, 'I can't put up with thith!'

Eric's face drew close to mine. 'Just don't get too friendly with him, Lucy, or he'll have you on your back quick-smart!' he said nastily, the insulting implication being that I had no say in the hypothetical assault. He strode off, hands in his pockets, and almost kicked one of the hens as he went.

Somewhat stunned, I sought time to process this surprising assault on my nerves and my honesty. Resting now in the shade of the silo where blessed solitude was assured, I meditated on the frightening change in Eric's personality. Growing up among nuns and with gentle-mannered Father Kline as a patriarchal figure, I had been insulated and never imagined I would know so severe a psychological battering as I had recently received.

In the emotional aftershock, I sat there on the ground, completely still, like a forlorn figure in a painting, and stared unseeing at the scurrying honey-ants. Eventually, the hour for evening chores and the changing column of shade from the silo nudged me to make a tentative move. Again, I had to brave our quarters now, the last place I wished to enter. Nevertheless, I mounted the two steps and went inside.

I was surprised by the change in Eric's manner but equally disconcerted by its suddenness. He had made a pot of tea and was on the point of coming to look for me when he saw my approach. He evinced shame and contrition and hovered about, seeming eager to please me. I was unreceptive to overtures of conciliation and could not yet even look at him. We sat at the table and spoke in a desultory manner, almost shyly, to one another, both carefully ignoring the combustible subject of his attack.

After lunch, we returned to our respective work. That night, everything seemed sweet again—to Eric, at least—but I was still inwardly bleeding. Entering the remorseful stage that always followed his mistreatment, he beseeched me to forgive him for misjudging his 'darling wife.'

Eric looked at me imploringly. 'I'm sorry, Lucy; I don't know what comes over me sometimes. I'm a typical green-eyed monster, I suppose,' he admitted rather childishly to elicit contradiction. 'I love you so much, Lucy,' he quickly said when I didn't respond, 'and I think I'm scared that you'll fall for someone better than me.'

In that final, honest statement, I recognised an inferiority fixation, the legacy of his father's ill-treatment. I saw the genuine need for reassurance in my husband's anguished face, and gently I gave it. Then, after re-telling me the story of his deprived childhood, he began to resurrect his oft-mentioned yen for a son.

In the short time we had shared our marriage bed, nothing had happened to procure this dream of his, and I began to wonder if there was something physically amiss in him or me. However, owing to my altered feelings, I didn't favour bringing a child into an atmosphere of see-sawing emotions. Indeed, after his tantrum over the truck, the mere mention of starting a family seemed ludicrous!

At the beginning of our romance, Eric had indeed presented an appealing veneer of himself, or perhaps we brought out the best in each other. However, as the months passed, the minuscule cracks appeared and grew into fractures. At first, I didn't want to acknowledge them, deeming even cumulative incidents too small to warrant a notice.

But minor became major, and inevitably our relationship lost its shine. Eric began to chip away at my self-esteem. He criticised my cooking and how I arranged my hair and cruelly mocked my lisp. Even the click of my busy knitting needles tortured his nerves. Indeed, it seemed I didn't possess a single redeeming feature.

I knew I should soon break away from Eric and try to resume my old life. However, by turning my back on the convent and Sister Casima, I had forfeited the right to the dear nun's solicitude. Consequently, the convent became an improbable option, so I continued to ponder what I had better do. But before I found a solution to my dilemma, our circumstances suddenly changed.

Already experiencing the scarcities imposed on everyone by the Depression, and feeling the effects of the drought and failed crops, the farmer became drawn into a financial crisis beyond his power to resolve. Expressing regret, Mr Bennet informed his employees that he had no alternative but to recruit family members to help save the farm. He therefore had to reduce the number of current workers, and Eric and Lucy Chadwick were among them.

That was the nearest I ever came to leaving my husband. As I packed my bag, Eric's alter ego, his chameleon nature, again became active. How fervently he entreated for a return of my love! How would he exist without me? And then it was 'us.' Where could we go? What would happen to us? Such was the changeable tenor of his supplication. Petitioning to a tender heart, Eric used his well-honed psychological power to soften my previously hardened intentions.

Thus, united in our misery, we fell prey to the human need for comfort, and when he appealed to me with kindness and with utter need kindling his features, he gradually gained my surrender.

Influenced by the social code of the day, I justified my weakness with a placating self-reminder. It was *for better or for worse*, and *strong couples stick together through thick and thin*. Such were the maxims uttered by women such as Lucy

Chadwick when the nightmare of procuring a divorce was beyond stressful, and financial support non-existent. It seemed easier to endure.

Although I thought I couldn't bear it, I *did* bear it with a revised attitude. 'All right, we'll try again, make a new start, follow the other folk who are now out of work.'

Like them, we would build a makeshift dwelling on the vacant land along the beach dunes. We bought a tent, packed up our scant belongings, and good Mr Bennet drove us to our selected spot at the beach. Indeed, it was almost exciting!

6

THE SHACK BY THE SEA

Surprisingly, Eric and I became almost content. Pioneering, a new experience for us, seemed oddly exciting at first. So with this impetus, we threw our energies into the construction of a neat shack with the materials scrounged from the local tip. Other settlers came by to offer friendship and help if we needed advice or any materials they could spare. They were good people, those struggling men and women, and I liked them all. However, Eric, who had never integrated with the farmworkers, retreated into his sulky loner character again and warned me to 'freeze off' our beach settlement neighbours.

Gradually, we were left alone. Paradoxically, Eric's previous sense of purpose and well-being, engendered by our home-building activities, began to wane, and the novel undertakings of equipping and living in our little place lost their appeal. My husband was a worker and *needed* to work. Once he had become bored with fishing, swimming, and walking along the beach with me, he fell again into his old habit of drinking alcohol.

Unlike thrifty me, my husband hadn't saved any of his earnings from the farm and spent without thought for the future. By some covert means, Eric procured various questionable concoctions of home-brew, and increasingly he left the shack and wandered off to some destination unknown to me to drink with friends. I discovered that some were women, so I wasn't surprised when he stayed out all night. Then the dark side of Eric's nature began to re-emerge, and with it came a return of his rages and insulting accusations.

We had experienced happiness in fleeting episodes, but now it was lying stone-dead and would never be resurrected. Gradually, bad sank to worse, and increasingly I wore and tried to hide the bruises of Eric's drunken temper. I shrank from seeking outside help, for it seemed preferable and wiser to remain alone on those nights when he didn't come home. I soon learnt the futility of asking him where and with whom he had been.

Hostilities escalated to a terrifying, volcanic head that final evening when Eric brutally twisted my arm. I realised then the imminent danger I faced and felt utterly relieved to watch him lurch away. I hoped never to see him again.

After Eric's departure, the seclusion of the primitive sanctuary lent itself to quietude and comfort. With the wretched bondage severed and the assurance that my husband was well away from our shack, I used the time and freedom to return to the simple activities that always gave me gentle pleasure.

I took stock of my possessions—a reasonably comfortable bed, a table and chair, and sundry items. The dwelling also sheltered my precious journals, with my saved pound notes concealed within some pages, and in that ambience of peace, the muse looked over my shoulder and provided a revised flow of inspiration to write. But there were nights when I fearfully imagined that every noise signified Eric's return.

* * *

Autumn had been beautiful that year, with softer sunshine and colourful leaves, and by the power of contrast, I see now that I was moderately content, living alone in my shack at the height of the Great Depression. But then it became even more evident that World War II was almost upon us.

'Hitler's stirring up trouble,' grumbled an old-timer I sometimes encountered at the communal water tap. 'That puppeteer Goebbels has got him believing he's God. Yeah, there's strife coming, and we'll be drawn into it again, Lucy, no two ways about it,' was his doleful prophecy, sharply tanged with garlic.

'Well, *you* won't have to fight again, Bill,' I said cheerfully.

'Nah, I'll have one foot in the grave by then. But mind you, I could still give 'em a run for their money!' he joked, withdrawing his foot.

The old fellow's bucket had filled, and I held mine under the running tap. He raised his hat to me, revealing the bald convexity of his head—moon-white, never having felt the sun.

'Well, hooroo, Lucy! Gunna brew a cuppa tea now,' Bill said and strolled off towards his tent at the end of the path.

As my bucket filled, I watched the bow-legged old soldier approaching his humble canvas home. I contemplated how eagerly some older men talked about the imminent war—perhaps because of remembered camaraderie or their exemption from service with their best days past. My interpretation was cynical, I suppose, but that was how the thought occurred then.

Many similar tents and shacks dotted the grassed stretch parallel to the beach. There, in the lee of the high dunes, people and dwellings were spared from the stinging sand and salt spray whipped up by the east wind. Tents, of course, were the most vulnerable of shelters to the vagaries of the weather. However, some buildings also were decidedly flimsy, with walls made only of hessian stretching around bush poles but at least rendered waterproof by a coating of lime mixed with fat.

Potato bags or tar paper held some huts together, equally fragile. However, the more substantial rough scantlings made the best dwellings. Men gleaned the materials from the nearby inactive sawmill. These sturdier shacks were reasonably watertight, roofed in the large slabs of bark from the stringybark trees and left in the bush by the redundant fence-post splitters.

They were a hardy lot, the shanty folk of the Depression. Resilience and resourcefulness were their greatest acquisitions. How sincerely I admired them! Many were mothers who, although thankful for their meagre comforts, were nevertheless burdened by the constant worry about the inadequate supply of food for their children. Some succumbed to severe emotional depression, worrying about where their weary men might be.

'Jim's tramping the "long paddock," y' know, Lucy,' said Mrs Henry, who now looked after her husband's shop. 'He's trying for work on, I dunno how many properties along the back roads—somewhere out west of Forbes, I think. That's where he posted the last letter, anyway.'

She wrapped newspaper around my half-loaf of bread, passed it over the counter, and her eyes widened as she took the large flathead I had caught that morning. 'And I dunno what he can scrounge to eat, poor blighter. Lord, I'm so worried about him! Sick with worry I am, Lucy.'

Similar anxiety loomed over almost all the shack dwellers whose menfolk were away seeking work and also food to sustain them while they searched. I was spared this concern. I now knew where my faithless man was and who was with him … and I hoped they both starved!

Doubtless, if others had discerned my predicament, my label would quickly become 'the deserted wife in the last shack.' However, I told no one. I wanted no sympathy, for I was free! A new kind of contentment and a novel sense of liberty gradually seeped into my being. I couldn't call it happiness, for I believed that luxury was beyond my reach.

So feeling secure in that crude shack of which I was so fond, I drew a daily delight from the ocean and the warm sand under my feet. It was a beautiful stretch of the coastline, and I spent my early mornings and late afternoons swimming, catching fish and crabs for Mrs Henry, and gathering pipis for the billycan.

I found further delight in joining other shanty dwellers in their quest for blackberries. Delicately, with finger and thumb, we pinched them off the prickly bushes that grew alongside the foot-worn track past the tents and shacks. Walking some evenings, we took the track threading between gum trees to the store and bought our essentials before it closed. Occasionally, I paused to chatter with the other women, who traded news and gossip, and this social contact gave me enjoyment, but mostly I kept to myself. Indeed, it was common for a day to pass without my seeing anyone.

The creative area of my brain was again beginning to function. I wanted to recapture my passion for writing and found deep pleasure in recording in my journal the daily activities, highlighted by anecdotes from other shack-dwellers previously befriended and of whose plights I had become acquainted.

In contrast to this fulfilment, and in an effort to retain and nurture the sense of inviolacy of my new situation, I often reflected upon that last day when Eric had twisted my arm behind my back until I thought it would wrench from its socket. The dreadfulness of that assault evoked a powerful depiction worthy of recording, accentuating how he had changed from an amiable young man to a belligerent drunkard.

Ironically, the exercise soothed me and, at the same time, stirred a renewed appreciation of my autonomous status. However, there was a thorn in the womb of this newly conceived complacency. It was this: I couldn't entirely banish the insult of Eric's last salvo, 'You're on your own now, and good riddance, you barren bitch!'

I was inured to the crudity, but the term 'barren' stung me to the quick, invading the guarded part of my psyche that usually shielded me from such sorrowing allusions. Eric had planted that seed during an argument, nourished it with reminders, and watched it grow. And how it rankled me! I wanted to punish him for this emotional cruelty and his duplicity, but I was more intent on seeing him go, relieved to watch him shamble off towards the silhouette of *her* waiting near the road. Vengefully, I hoped she would soon meet his other, malignant self and know first-hand what I had suffered.

    Returning indoors, I pettishly snatched up Eric's enamel mug—as though it were an embodiment of him. I felt the strongest urge to run down over the beach and cast it out into the wild surf. But common sense and poverty prevailed. I shoved the mug out of sight on the shelf, there to remain until the practical need of it purged its power of association.

7

THE ACCIDENT

During my teens, I enjoyed horse-riding lessons, and it wasn't long before the instructor reinforced my modest notion that I had a natural affinity with horses. My small frame was light in the saddle, and the horse exhibited great enjoyment in a canter and, later, the freedom to gallop. On occasions of irresponsible impulse, I dared even to ride bare-back an obliging old granny-mare.

Sometime after my perfidious cretin of a husband had left me at the beach shack to frisk off with his female predator counterpart (it relieved me somewhat to regard them as such), I left my shack to take a walk through the bushland with its diversity of wildflowers. Still distraught over Eric's brutality, my feet set a faster pace to help work off some of my anger energy until wearying of the exercise. Aimlessly, I sauntered along a track, seeking distraction in the antics of curious birds while wondering what I had better do now that Eric was safely out of my life.

My options differed widely in their nature. I could remain in the shack by the much-loved tempestuous ocean and, free of Eric's antisocial presence, embrace that marginalised community of humpy dwellers whose ethos was to look out for each other. Importantly, the store and provisions were only a pleasant three-minute walk from my home.

Of course, if 'humble pie' were on my menu, there was the option of a contrite return to Sister Casima and the familiarity of my old home. Idealising my homecoming, I envisioned it as an all-embracing, forgiving event, bringing to mind an evocative line of Maudie Sullivan's parlour song:

'Like the black sheep of old, I'll come back to the fold.'

Benefits beckoned. Once I had confessed my lately accrued sins to Father Kline, the bestowal of sweet absolution would soothe like a paternal pat on the head from the Divine hand. And afterwards, while enjoying the state of grace under a new halo, wayward Lucy would enjoy a return of acceptance, comfort, and the convent's protection.

Once a Catholic, always a Catholic, I thought wryly as I walked along. The convent or the beach? *To stay or not to stay—* that was my dilemma.

I wandered through the bush, deeply pondering these options, but then, quite abruptly, the sight of a bay horse some distance through the trees stopped me. I approached as quietly as the dried leaves and sticks allowed and saw that it was the local mare I had several times observed. She was a creature of the forest and quite ribby, many years having passed since her taming, and the free spirit she evinced in her proud and watchful eye attracted me. Furthermore, like me, the animal appeared to be abandoned, and that realisation struck a responsive chord in my psyche.

The horse wasn't skittish, and after a while of gentle, whispered persuasion, her confidence grew, and I led her to a log. From that elevation, I was able to throw my leg over her bony back, and we rode off westward along a scarcely discernible forester's track. *Later, we'll head eastward towards home*, ran my thoughts as we ventured further into the forest. I intended to tether the dear old horse on the grassy patch next to the shack and take good care of her.

However, the mare sensed no inkling of my benevolent adoption plans. Exhilarated by the exercise and coming upon an open track, she broke into an unstoppable gallop that belied her gaunt appearance. I had to use all my strength to hang on and dodge the overhead hazards. That was my last memory of the horse. A low branch had sent me thudding to the stone-pocked ground, and there, among the bush debris, I lost consciousness.

8

THE BARBED WIRE PRISON

As I emerged from my insentient state, the first foggy awareness of excruciating pain in my thigh registered along with a throbbing that was knocking my brain about. When I could tolerate the gradual lift of eyelids, I found myself recumbent on a high bed in a strange building, smelling dogs and burning gum leaves. My eyes moved slowly in their stinging sockets, from left to right, upwards and down, and I saw that the stout walls were made of mud bricks. I pondered a moment on the strangeness of that; there were no such dwellings near the village or Rivers Bend. I guessed then that this house must be situated in a deep part of the forest unknown to me.

Completely disoriented, I yearned to be away from things unfamiliar and back again in the open space close to my seaside shack.

No one would have noticed me walking into the forest, much less that I had found a horse. No one could have known that it had carried me into the wilderness—certainly much farther than I'd have gone had I not lost control. I wondered if old Bill or the shopkeeper, Mrs Henry—indeed, any person from the distant humpies—had happened to drop by my shack that day. If so, they might have assumed that I was off on one of my frequent bush walks or had gone to the distant town, Rivers Bend, for a while. Not a soul would imagine that I was stranded in this isolated place.

I listened but heard no human sound. I tried to sit up but immediately fell back, struck by the pain in my thigh and the throb in my head. I grew frightened. Lying there in this strange bushland dwelling, utterly confounded by this seismic change of events, I grew impatient to learn the identity of my rescuer and where this person now was. With a dry mouth and tender bladder, I winced and raised myself on an elbow. My gaze rested on the staircase, and I wondered who, or what, was up there.

Stretching my neck, I gained enough height to allow a curious survey through the window above the bed. I was alarmed to observe that the dwelling was fenced off from the thick bush by an unusually high barbed-wire barrier. It struck me with full force then that whoever had found me in the forest after my fall might now be my jailer.

I waited and listened. Relieved that my leg wasn't broken, I eased my body down from the bed, crept painfully to the doorway, and looked out. It was a shock to observe the extent of the all-encompassing tall and sinister barbed wire fencing. I became suddenly overwhelmed by despair and panic, convinced I would never again see my old home waiting there by the ocean.

Hesitantly, with every movement torture, I ventured out a short distance from the cottage into the white glare of sunshine and stopped still. Across the paddock, I saw a massive figure in overalls. Three dogs exploded into a salvo of barking and bounded towards me. My limbs froze; my heart banged. The dogs' master, at the chopping block, quickly turned and whistled them back. They instantly obeyed him.

The big man stared at me. After my moment of paralysis had eased, I saw what I desperately sought—a small building among some fruit trees further down the incline from the cottage. When I pointed my arm, he understood and nodded, then turned back to his work. Gratefully, I hobbled there as fast as possible while trying to ignore my screaming thigh. The building's amenity was primitive, but it didn't matter; I only wanted relief.

Retracing my steps a few minutes later, I called out, hating my lisp, as always, to the man. 'Where am I, pleathe?'

He swung the axe hard into the stump and walked across the yard towards me. Again my legs grew rigid, and I stared apprehensively.

'Thank you for helping me,' I said as bravely and pleasantly as I could, hoping to establish a criterion of tentative friendliness that would improve my chances of going home.

I was surprised when only a few masculine sounds, which might have been words, erupted from his mouth. He raised his arm to indicate the quaint house with its attic roof and gestured for me to follow him there, but he didn't explain anything. And so, entirely bewildered and afraid, I entered the strange world of this big man's silence.

He poured water into the hanging kettle and went about stoking the fire, frequently glancing back at me as I looked around the room. Indeed, now that I was mobile, his eyes began to watch my every move, and his dogs followed me around. My love of animals, especially dogs, has always been a dominant trait of my nature. However, I was utterly afraid of these huge, intimidating creatures.

The man, busy at the table slicing meat, turned and indicated with the knife the other chair, which was to become my place at the table. The meal didn't look pleasing, and my expectation of its tastiness was low. Lacking an appetite, I couldn't eat the boiled potatoes and the unfamiliar meat he offered. I sat there, passive and silent and close to despair, vowing to attempt an escape from this nightmare before my impaired rationality entirely deserted me.

While the man had his head down eating his meal, I made another inspection of my present environment. The building, which I euphemistically label 'cottage,' was a single-roomed rustic edifice supported by bush poles, some blackened by smoke from the fireplace. The substantial mud brick walls were a foot thick, I estimated. The worn thoroughfares of the timber floor between pieces of rough but robust homemade furniture bore testimony to the scuffing of boots over many years. Above, where a ceiling might be, I could see the underside of the attic flooring, the attic accessible by steep, rough-hewn stairs.

The large bed stood opposite the open fireplace at the other end of the single-roomed cottage. Above the bedhead, a window, semi-opaque with the residue of dirt and smoke, allowed only scant light to infiltrate the room. It was darkish and Spartan, the dwelling, and malodorous and depressing—made worse by the odour of the dogs.

After banking up the fire that first night, the man turned his dark eyes upon me again. He handed me a bottle of water and gestured towards the staircase. 'Bed,' I thought he said, and he lifted his arm to indicate the door at the top of the stairs. Apprehensively and cautiously, my feet mounted the steps, my thigh throbbing. I became alarmed when the man followed me up to the door. I entered the attic, relieved that he remained on the other side. He closed the door, and the bolt slid home.

Wide-eyed, I peered around in the dimness. I was alone in that wide roof space, a 'room' of extraordinary simplicity, more significant in area but not much better than the beach shacks. My eyes immediately went to the apex windows, lit by the dying sun.

'Wetht,' I said aloud and with satisfaction that I could orient my position with the points of the compass. It was the first logical thought relating to the concept of escape that had come to me since regaining consciousness after my accident. My headache had eased, but I suspected that my still somewhat-muddled brain had not yet grasped the full implication of my predicament.

There was no way of calculating exactly how long I had lain on the man's bed downstairs, but I assumed it was still the same day because the bedding was dry. Unfortunately, since my acquaintance with the man's outdoor privy, I had swallowed too much water, and my nuisance organ was again increasing the strength of its signal. I could no longer ignore it. The kerosene tin near the attic window provided improvisation, a blessed relief, and a lesson in humility. (Even at the beach's humpy settlement, the community had access to a clean lavatory.)

There was no bed in the attic, but on the floor where the roof stole the headspace lay an improvised mattress, merely a rough palliasse. Closer inspection revealed that it was a huge, stitched hessian sack stuffed with raw fleece, some of which protruded through the gaps of the uneven needlework. The quantity of wool suggested the shearing of two animals. I could smell the overpowering odour of the sheep that had yielded up their coats and could see the long, wide stain of wool grease where, over time, the pressure of someone's body had forced it through the coarse weave.

A thick wire was stretched across the underside of the ridge pole. An old calico sheet, its folds united by white swathes of cobwebs, hung carelessly from it, and further along, several nails might have served as hangers for clothes. I peered around. Directly opposite the mattress, two wooden boxes occupied the space against the sharp angle where the roof met the floor. They contained a thin, grey blanket, overalls, a flannel shirt, and a woollen coat that had endured many years of toil, tempest, and moths.

From the window, I could just see in the fading light the sprawling paddocks enclosed in numerous strands of barbed wire. Immediately before the west fence, the glitter of water had turned golden with the sun's decline. If my knowledge of topography still served, it seemed logical to assume that the stream was a natural run-off from the distant mountain. I recognised the unique birdcage shape of that mountain top, still verdant against the sky, and it struck me then that somewhere vaguely opposite was the location of my coastal shanty home. From that ocean viewpoint, the high asymmetrical 'pyramid' was perceived only as an impressive shape on the horizon—but bluish.

My mind was clearing, and I speculated: How many miles did that colour change indicate? What distance alters the human perception of colour? How significant are the changes in atmospheric gases? How far away, then, is home?

Good—the synapses were still zapping away in their cranium cradle!

As darkness fell, I first sat cross-legged on the floor and then stretched my length on the dusty planks to ease the ache in my back. It took further time and pacing before I could reconcile myself with the environment, and I had to fight an almost overwhelming revulsion for the bedding before attempting to seek any comfort from it. Nevertheless, when weariness had weakened my defences, I gingerly reached for the sheet from the overhead wire line. By candlelight, I searched for spiders and then placed the sheet and my unwilling, aching limbs upon the revolting bed.

It was surprisingly comfortable! Yet I lay for hours trying to ignore the smell, tossing and crying in my overwhelming despair. I wished to fall asleep but feared that some dreaded incubus would invade my dreams. Time passed slowly; theories jostled for prominence. All my senses told me I was not dreaming, and my mind, much clearer now, began to speculate again on my unconscious state of that day and to evaluate all that had happened before.

Now, stuck in this strange, wild place, my musings dwelt longingly on my home, snug in a world of ordinary human beings, of friends, of freedom, where I could come and go at will. My refuge was indeed humble, yet beauteous nature surrounded its corrugated tin walls. The expansive ocean vista inspired awe as it emphasised my human smallness, and the movement of waves crashing or gently folding over the white sand produced music that only lovers of the sea can appreciate.

Eventually, these nostalgic thoughts became sufficiently detached to allow me to sink into an exhausted sleep. I knew no more until woken by the startling, rasping chorus of roosters. They were juvenile, managing only half of the expected crowing heraldry. Undoubtedly, all were destined for the cooking pot—all but the full-throated old warrior that sired them.

9
ESCAPE PLAN

I waited and listened for sounds indicating the approach of my jailer, now lumbering around in the kitchen below. I tested the door. It was still locked. Belatedly I gave silent thanks to whichever divinity decreed I should survive that this rough man hadn't visited me during the night. The gruff sound of his voice and the barking of dogs sharpened my hearing and rattled every nerve. I listened harder, my heartbeats thumping my ribs. Presently, the stair treads creaked under ponderous feet. The bolt grated, and the big man stooped to negotiate the doorway.

'Dinna!' the deep voice commanded. The man nodded several times, which seemed to be his usual mannerism. He glanced around at the unaltered arrangement of the room and then pointed down the stairs. 'Dinna,' he repeated, but in a softer tone. I later learnt that this word did duty for *meal*, *food*, and *eat*, regardless of the time of day.

I stood there, still afraid of him despite his gentler voice. 'But I'm not hungry!' I protested, in as benign an attitude as possible, and continued to stare at him. 'I would rather go home, pleathe.'

He seemed unable to understand me and said what sounded like 'essen' and then 'dinna' again, repeating the arm gesture. What I could see of the face behind the dark beard was ruddy—with impatience at my stupefaction, I assumed—and in this attitude, he waited for me to precede him down the stairs. I was reluctant to cross the kitchen floor where the three smelly guards sprawled, and the man nudged me, though not roughly, past them and towards the table to my first austere breakfast. It was the leftover potatoes and unidentifiable meat I had refused last night.

My skull still ached from the blow it had received when I fell from the horse, and I sat there, head in hand, and stared at the meal. Then I felt my heart jolt. The man approached and peered at the wound above my ear, which he had already inspected, along with whatever else he had observed while attending to my unconscious self.

'Bad?' he asked with a sympathetic tone softening his voice, and mutely I stared back at the bearded face, so uncomfortably close. With a sudden movement (I learnt he could move fast when he wished), he crossed to the wash-up dish at the window, wrung out a soapy rag, and returned to my chair. 'Blut!' I thought was what he exclaimed, and I felt blood trickling down my neck.

Bracing myself, I submitted to his ministrations, hoping he was unaware that my chest jerked with each loud heart thump when his fingers pattered the wound. As I had been surprised by the comfort of the ammonia-smelling mattress, now I was equally surprised by his attentive gentleness.

Later that day, completely overwhelmed by the wretched bondage, I became sufficiently brave to protest and demand that he take me to any track that would lead to civilisation, or at least to where he had found me.

'Why are you keeping me here?' I cried. 'I want to go home! *Pleathe* take me to the road! You are treating me like a criminal,' I almost screamed. 'You have no right to keep me here!' This passionate surge of words seemed to bewilder the odd individual. I checked my red-hot emotions and, catching my breath, glared at him, expecting an angry response. But he merely stared as though struck by the significant change in my former docile-seeming manner.

On subsequent occasions, although he must have understood my angry bewilderment, appeals, and hand gestures, he nevertheless seemed unable to grasp the meaning of my words. It occurred to me that perhaps he felt reluctant to admit understanding, a pretext to justify keeping me there. But now, as he seemed to subside into momentary puzzlement again, I remembered 'Blut' and 'Essen' and thought he might be German. I regretted my outburst.

Towards evening, despite the memory of the awful breakfast, hunger began to assert its punishing self. But the potatoes this time were hot and good, and there was also a spinach-like vegetable, which I suspected to be a common weed. Those greens, and the taste and texture of the meat, were utterly alien to me, but I forced myself to swallow and tried not to guess what

I was eating. My stomach protested the arrival of the fatty meat, and slight nausea soon followed, but at least the cook seemed pleased that I had eaten a full meal.

At length he gestured towards the wash-up dish, indicating that domestic drudgery constituted women's work, and I qualified. I supposed that was fair enough, but I didn't realise then that for as long as I remained a prisoner, my duties would include outdoor work: milk the goats, bucket water from the stream, wash the clothes there, gather kindling, and also prepare the bland meals each day. Later, I so wished for onions and herbs to disguise the wild flavour of the meat I cooked, but at least the potatoes were 'normal food.'

As I struggled to reconcile sleep with the odious mattress, my need to escape became more desperate, but at least I had Cat to comfort me and keep me sane. And oh, how I loved and needed her! There were times when I was crying and she came close to stare at me, touch me with her little paw, and then bump her head to my face. I knew she understood my feelings and was trying to console me. Now, stroking my purring companion fondly, I promised to take her with me.

Sometimes I felt worn out and older than my years. There, in the attic prison, I held a metaphorical mirror to myself and saw a childless woman of slight build and brown hair. The picture appeared quite bedraggled now, for so much had happened to me. Until my accident, I was content to wait out the Depression's aftermath in my beach shack and then seek work again if work could be found. Naturally, my first choice was to continue at *The Rivers Bend Weekly*; my second was to do office work or serve behind a counter in one of the town's stores.

Understandably, my speech impediment lessened my employment options in some workplaces. Indeed, I had already been subjected to derisive remarks and mockery of my lisping speech, and these incidents effectively turned my thoughts back to the comparatively insular occupation of writing. I longed for my journals and writing effects: pencils, pens, ink, and paper. Reading and losing myself in writing had become synonymous with solace and reliable, non-judgmental company—books and the ocean.

* * *

While reflecting on the violence of my husband, it struck me how quickly I had fallen prey to the dominance of another man—my 'rescuer'—and I feared I had slipped from a hot frying pan. I contemplated my jailer—not young, but nor was he middle-aged. I also wondered about his startling bursts of impatience, which very much unsettled me and sometimes sent Cat streaking up her pear tree refuge.

The big man's tendency towards irritation, and sometimes momentary vacuity, often was evident, and it began to seem that a wide gap existed between his mental and actual ages. I knew to take advantage of this, to dismiss my negative thoughts and draw positives from the situation. Thus, my wits would help me to escape from him. To this end, I affected acceptance and subservience, and he began to abandon his surveillance.

Over weeks, he gradually withdrew the restrictions imposed upon my daily activities. Eventually, under his occasional glances, I was free to explore the three or four acres of the home yard surrounding the cottage. I had changed my tactic and now affected the manner of a quiet and trembling creature that jumped at every sound. My angry mouth no longer screamed at him, and I made no new demands to be set free. Docility was my pretence, and I demonstrated compliance and acceptance, while inwardly my brain worked overtime on my plan to escape.

I was keenly aware that this man had not once struck me as my husband might have done. Indeed, there was a gentleness about my jailer, paradoxical though that concept was. No doubt he now accepted that I was resigned with spirit broken, yet I had not succumbed to any negative influence. On the contrary, my mind, energy, and determination were even more robust, and I resolved to use those guarded attributes until I was free. He eventually would be the prisoner—a prisoner of the law.

Every night, I whisper-chanted my new mantra: *Freedom requires patience. I will escape.* However, at times the harsh reality overwhelmed me. Perhaps had I even conquered the dangerous fence, the man, noticing my absence too soon, would send the dogs after me. I was trapped, and my stalwart attitude, so carefully nurtured, sometimes deserted me when the dreadful thought struck: *Will I grow old and mute and stupid in this Godforsaken concentration camp?* Perhaps I would never again see Sister Casima—nor the beautiful ocean.

To counter attacks of depression in my present situation, I often visualised myself back in my humble little seaside home.

There I would put pen to paper to record every aspect of this outrage for the benefit of the law courts. If only I now had writing paper and a pencil!

My jailer was always busy preparing skins for trading, tending the farm animals, or chopping firewood. Sometimes he worked at chipping out tussock grass and other weeds that threatened to overrun his paddocks, seldom glancing my way. At evening, he set rabbit traps and at night, gunshots rang out when he hunted wallabies in the bush—eventful, I suppose, but even so, my life had become entirely devoid of the simplest joys. I endured the daylight hours through the particulars of domestic events and eagerly sought nightfall and oblivion in sleep. However, the will to escape overrode everything. And so, gradually retrieving the remnant of my natural stoicism, I began a cautious mental climb.

10

TRADING THE FURS

Time elapsed with the emerging and departing of the sun, and each day passed with a monotonous sameness of activities that made me feel robotic. During my permitted afternoon walks, I searched every inch of the seven-strand barbed wire fence and the four locked gates for weakness but found none. However, my spirits lifted somewhat when I located the 'chook' pen in a tea-tree-enshrouded yard near a dam. As expected, there was a gathering of hens scratching in the dirt, and I counted eight, obviously not yet laying. I fed them every day on hard corn grits and table scraps, talking to them as they pounced on the food. I longed to find a few eggs in their grass-filled nesting boxes.

Our joint warden usually released the fowls about mid-morning to forage in the nearby scrub. But occasionally, circling eagles spying from the altitudes threatened their liberty, and it became my duty to scan the skies every few minutes whenever the hens were foraging. Cat became increasingly companionable to me during this time. I welcomed the occasional brush of her soft fur against my legs and the sweet way she looked up at me, meowing in a querying tone.

'Yeth, I know what you're thinking, my darling,' I crooned. 'I'll get you out of here thoon.' In the meantime, I turned my thoughts to finding a befitting name for my regal companion, even though the man only called her 'Cat.'

The time eventually arrived for skins to be traded for supplies. At the first dull light of day, the man freed me in time to complete my chores, visit the leaning lavatory down the yard, and bathe in privacy in the tinkling stream behind the mass of curtaining willows. Refreshed, I gathered food oddments and port-bottle of water, ample sustenance for my day locked in the attic and superfluously guarded by the dogs in the kitchen.

Banished to the confines of the attic, I leaned out of the window to watch, but the man didn't walk westward. It was impossible, therefore, to observe the direction of his departure to learn which of the three bush tracks he had taken. The sun, barely risen as he left, gradually westered to sit glowing reddish-orange upon the bushland horizon when he returned. I estimated that his walk would have taken roughly ten or eleven hours overall had he not stopped anywhere.

'But which way?' I addressed the vital question to Cat. 'How are we ever going to get out of thith hell-hole if I can't even find the right track?' I asked her as though she had human understanding and emotions.

She sat there on our smelly mattress and looked back at me, probably perplexed by the voluble noise erupting from my usually closed mouth. I knelt to caress her lovely, almost orange-hued fur, which always set her purring.

'You're coming with me, darling Cat, and we'll live in freedom at the beautiful beach. I'll catch fith to eat and give you milk to drink, and we'll be very happy together.'

I was talking to her as though she were a child, but often I spoke on a more elevated level, discussing all kinds of subjects, including the worrying threat of another war. She appeared to like my voice, even with the accursed lisp, and lifted and lowered her head with each smoothing stroke of my hand as I softly spoke to her.

Shortly after the big man's return, he unlocked my door, and I descended the stairs to light the fire and to observe what provisions he had bought. I had tried to indicate the need for soap, flour, sugar, salt, and tea, but I doubted he could understand, much less remember everything besides items for the farm.

The initial consonants of the items I requested didn't lend themselves to a simple mnemonic, and there needed to be something visibly available to write with or on. How could he live without paper? I had longed to conceal a message within a list that I assumed he would hand to the trader, for I suspected that not only was my jailer semi-mute but was unable to recognise any English words.

Therefore, I was surprised to discover that he had remembered the groceries, and I observed him afresh. Again, I wondered why he couldn't speak and how he managed to communicate at the trading post, or whatever the establishment was, where he swapped skins for provisions. I assumed the rabbit skins were destined for the Akubra factory in Sydney but couldn't work out where the goat and kangaroo hides would go. More importantly, I longed to know which track he had taken that morning bearing the heavy sacks, for there, of course, lay my escape route.

Among the groceries was a tiny newspaper triangle stuck to a bar of soap. I held the bar firmly, carefully removed the paper scrap, and took the fragment to the window's light for scrutiny. It was a section of an advertisement for cod liver oil with a partial depiction of the fruity hat on Carmen Miranda's smiling head. I thought it so incongruous that on the reverse of the cheery paper scrap was a photograph of a swastika above goose-stepping soldiers. However, the associated print was disappointingly absent.

The swastika brought an unpleasant memory to me of something drunken Eric had said after reading incredible reports about the extermination of Jewish people. A snort of derision preceded his bigoted declaration: 'Ha! That's what we should do to the useless abos!' And I remembered the clout my cheek received when I fiercely defended Australia's much-maligned Indigenous people.

My shopper sat wearily at the table now and stretched out his long legs, and I noticed cobbler's pegs clinging to his socks and overalls. As I poured the fragrant, sugared tea into tin mugs, I realised none of these grasping seeds grew in the south paddock, for the goats ate everything, even the thorny blackberry vines.

How interesting! That meant it was either in the north or east direction that he had travelled.

This information inspired confidence. It halved the possibilities, doubled my chances, and reinforced my resolve to be patient and observant. Meanwhile, I had soft, white flour and salt for a damper and sugar for the tea. Later, if the man brought in a rabbit, I wouldn't boil it as usual but roast the tender pink meat with seasoned potatoes. The prospect of a meal that came closer to normal lifted my spirits a little.

A few days later, a violent storm thrashed the farm. The unlined roof was too close above my head in the attic, and the rain drummed deafeningly on the corrugated iron, seemingly for hours. It was terrifying, and I flinched with each resounding *boom*, sure that the end of the world would sound exactly so. At some time, well advanced into the night, there was a nerve-shredding crash. It had come from the east.

In the morning, all was sunshine. I dressed this time in the overalls and flannel shirt, for it was time to wash my green dress again. The aromatic scent of the she-oak needles and gum leaves in the fire, just lit, wafted up the stairs as the man unlocked my door. I went down to eat before beginning my work.

Later, while hanging the washing over the line between the cottage and shed, I peered at the thick bush and saw that it was a large bloodwood that had crashed down in the storm. The roots were thrust high towards the dense bush canopy, and I noticed they had heaved up mustard-coloured clay as the falling tree wrenched them from the deep earth. This knowledge was indeed useful.

A few weeks later, after the man returned from another trek for supplies, the soles of his boots carried a residue of the same clay into the house.

'Therefore,' I announced to my feline confidante, 'the way out of here ith along that particular track.'

I roughly calculated the time it had taken him to cover one way and knew how far I could walk in an hour. I estimated it would take me about six hours of energetic walking to reach civilisation if nothing impeded my progress. I visualised the ocean, the tent-and-shack community, and the blessed company of normal, friendly, *talking* people again. However, I didn't want to encounter or even think about my husband and his new woman.

With stealth, I began to prepare for my escape. I plotted carefully and patiently until confident of every detail's efficacy. A rope was needed to haul my limbs up and over that high, vicious barbed wire fence while my jailer was elsewhere distracted. I planned to tether Cat and slip her under the lowest strand if she let me. I had noticed earlier that a discarded goat skin was lying forgotten on a pile of rubbish behind the shed. Realising its potential for safely cushioning the top of the spiked fence, I resolved to fetch it at the first opportunity.

While attending my chores, I created plausible pretexts for venturing into the shed, Cat at my heels, but didn't find any rope the man wouldn't miss. The thought then struck me—I could make one! It wasn't difficult to fashion a spindle using three sticks and a potato (the blessed nun who brought me up had taught me many such skills). After that, I worked every evening, pulling a quantity of fleece from the mattress and spinning it into the first ply of my rope.

Suddenly, there was so much to do. I felt strangely exhilarated by the potential reward of the task ahead. Now, rather than struggling to reconcile my over-weary mind and body with sleep, I used the precious time to spin three lengths of wool, plaiting them to form a strong cord sufficient to straddle the fence or the equally treacherous gate.

Sometimes I worked well into the night and became adept at spinning by tactile means, but when the moon was bare and bright, I increased the time spent on this activity. Each morning I hid my 'rope' inside the mattress, and after working with it at night, the wool made a soft pillow, albeit somewhat smelly! Sleep came quickly, anyway.

Gradually, my outlook brightened. During the day, I incorporated exercise into every activity, ate larger meals, and moved about with increased energy. I was in training, mentally and physically—strength and endurance were the prerequisites for conquering the fence. Then a fast escape into the bush would initiate the long and arduous trek, carrying Cat and the necessities the entire distance to a public road.

The plan was contingent on good weather, but when the first opportunity arose, the rain slapped and thrashed, wretchedly continuing for days and temporarily deferring my long-awaited attempt for freedom. Bitterly disappointed, I nevertheless valued the delay to revise other possible eventualities and to improve my stamina. Moreover, it gave me time to modify a hessian sack by making a head-hole for Cat's comfort and a shoulder strap for mine.

Every night, before allowing sleep to descend, I visualised each step of my intended escape, with Cat snug in her bag and a supply of food and water in another. I would move stealthily at first, then faster until I could feel safe enough to slow the pace and rest. Earnestly, I prayed to whatever the dregs of my childhood perception of benevolent God still lingered within me for favourable weather and the opportunity to arrive soon. Now, at last, physically and confidently, I was ready.

Always before sinking into blessed sleep, my thoughts drifted yearningly over the sandhills and dunes to the ocean, sighing sonorously or crashing its breakers. Again I saw the trees on the headland bowing with the westerly wind towards the two blues of the seemingly spirit-level horizon. I envisaged the quaint outline of my lonely little home, snug in the dunes and waiting for me.

But was it a desperately naïve expectation that things would be the same as before? Yes, it was, but I needed to believe the shack would be waiting. Robbed, indeed—alas, my money!—for people had gathered so few possessions to themselves during the Depression, and I wouldn't blame anyone for scavenging from an abandoned dwelling. If no one had moved into my shack and the elements had not been too ravaging, I would again claim my right of possession. Otherwise, there would be another long walk to the convent in the more distant town, carrying Cat all the way. I prayed again that the shack and my few precious belongings would be waiting, most importantly, my journals filled with autobiographical writings. So if all went well, we'd be happy there, my little ginger friend and I.

Lying there on that odorous sheep bed, I somewhat complacently began reviewing my careful preparedness, and the possibility of becoming lost during the escape suddenly struck me. I sat up, fully awake now, and asked my appalled self, 'What if I came to a fork in the track and chose the wrong one? What if I end up even deeper in the wild?' The direst of fates now loomed in my imagination, chasing off all former confidence.

I focused on this thought—I had no idea where the track left the bush to emerge onto the main road. Nor could I recollect the existence of a skin trader or trading post, even in the distant vicinity of the shack dwellers. Indeed, no one had ever mentioned such an establishment. I was stuck in provincial obscurity, unaware of how much farther I would have to walk once I found a road to reach my old home. Nevertheless, I took comfort in knowing that my ragged sandshoes would tread the unknown final distance along a reasonably well-formed gravel road where there would be the heartening possibility of meeting a vehicle.

However, a belated thought occurred: Now that it was winter, how chilly would it be near the beach in just a tin shack? That realisation required much sensible consideration.

11

JOSEF

He seemed easily fooled, my jailer, and ironically of late, his manner suggested satisfaction that I had settled into life under his dominance. Although stealthily waiting for a chance to escape, I encouraged this belief by feigning contentment. The dogs no longer threatened me; I ceased fearing them, and my heart yielded. I had noticed how they often sat at their master's feet. I believed this hound worship spoke well of him. Furthermore, when the dogs' affection turned my way, I was obliged to reach and stroke them, drawing the man's smiling nods. The whipping tails and drooling red smiles were counter-productive to guard duty, but their god was well-pleased, and day by day, his watch over me relaxed.

 This large, strong man who held me in captivity differed from anyone I had ever met. Despite the yearning to gain the free side of the hazardous fence, I became increasingly curious to learn something about him and surrendered to that curiosity one evening.

'What ith your *name*?' I asked. He stared at me perplexedly, unaccustomed as he was to hearing words, or perhaps he had forgotten his name, I allowed. I didn't discount the possibility that he was, to some degree, mentally backward. However, this notion weakened as I acknowledged his capable farm management.

His brown eyes stared back entreatingly, as though eager to understand. I lightly slapped a hand to my chest. 'Luthy,' I said, my tongue playing mischief with the sibilance. 'Who are you?' I asked carefully and pointed again.

Before I could doubt him further, his eyes lit up, and a broad smile lifted his face's serious contours, revealing healthy white teeth. 'Yosef!' he exclaimed, shaking his head and laughing as though deriding his slow reaction. 'Yosef!' he repeated with a slap to his chest. Then, with marked elation, he carefully enunciated, 'Luthy … Yosef!' I noted how he pronounced Josef with the soft 'y' initial and deduced that he was indeed of the Germanic tribe.

Thus began my resolve to teach Josef some English, or to retrieve speech if a catastrophe had stolen it from him. However, I wasn't so elated as to forget my principal purpose. This teaching experiment was primarily an exercise to provide my brain with some mental stimuli until the time was right to attempt an escape.

The next day, Josef greeted me with, 'Luthy!' His tone and air were almost commanding. At the door, he pointed an arm towards the distant corner of the cottage paddock, where an apple tree spread its shade. In a heart-chilling moment, his hand grabbed my arm and led me there, my feet half-running to keep up with his strides. There was a weed-covered heap of smooth stones symmetrically arranged around the tree. 'Papa,' he said, and his expression told me all. I nodded and hoped he discerned sympathy in my face.

After a silent moment, he guided me farther along to where a smaller apple tree grew amid a similar collection of river stones. 'Mama,' he said solemnly, and I deduced by the comparative youth of the tree that his father had predeceased his mother by quite some years.

As I lay with Cat on our attic-room bed that night, I contemplated Josef's parents and longed to know what had caused their deaths. There was also the intrigue of why they had secured a lock to the attic door. The palliasse, of course, would have been Josef's bed, so the unsettling thought stirred: Was there something ominous I should know about this man? Indeed, somewhere in the mysterious territory of Josef's mind, there awaited a tragic or menacing story desperately needing to be told, and I was impatient to discover it. I remembered the anti-German indoctrination I had sometimes encountered and thought that perhaps the attic was used as a safe place in which to stow valuables when trouble threatened.

A yawn stretched my jaws to their limits. I turned on my side to snuggle up with the faithful little ginger body. Comfortable now and dismissing all thoughts of drama, my mind settled on the conviction that Josef's hard-working father, builder of the mud brick cottage, sheds, fences, and sundry smaller buildings, had likely died of a heart attack.

I realised that it was only Josef and his mum working the farm before the poor woman, equally hard-working, followed her husband to heaven—if such a place exists, added my cynical inner persona. How awful it must have been for Josef to be left alone for all those years and initially in a state of grief borne without the support of human solicitude! Finally, my thoughts fragmenting, I let myself slip away from awareness.

The winter solstice passed, and the daylight hours gradually lengthened. I had kept approximate track of the days by depositing the smooth, black seeds of wattle in the rusty sardine tins I found behind the shed. Each container represented one month. My head pulsed with questions, and I craved answers.

Josef had learnt to string essential words together, and his mood swings and bouts of frustrated impatience ceased. I realised that his changing temperaments were engendered by the maddening inability to communicate, as a child throws a tantrum for that reason. Moreover, he seemed less of a jailer figure now. His face wore a gentler expression, and he had become quieter in his movements about the room.

As I walked about the frosty paddock hugging myself against the July cold, I ran these new characteristics through my mind. They summoned an interesting challenge, and I rose to meet it determinedly. With newly found fervour, I resolved that as long as I was forced to remain with Josef, I would do my utmost to provide him with at least a rudimentary grasp of speech. Whether he would use it when I was gone would remain forever unknown to me.

* * *

I was surprised one day to find Josef digging a wide hole midway between the cottage and the east fence. The next day, he started shaping mud, straw, and sand into mud bricks, laying them in the sun to dry and covering them each evening with a tarpaulin. I was intrigued. With fragments of distorted German and English, he explained how he would build a meat house on the site for the salted meat. What a shock that was! This project would take a long time, and his working there every day would significantly delay my escape attempt. I sank into a state of gloom.

Early one morning, Josef prepared to make another journey to trade skins. I cautiously framed my lisping appeal. 'May I come with you thith time, Jothef?' It was tantamount to admitting that I would break away when I reached a public road.

He had read flight in my face and in the supplicating tone of my words, and he cast upon me a dumbly astounded look, almost as though I had struck him. 'You—you *leave* me?'

I sensed that my eyes were pleading. 'Jothef, I want to go home,' and even as I spoke, his head began swaying sideways to negate the unsettling idea.

Indeed, he seemed stricken and looked at me searchingly. His hand reached forward, and a finger bestowed feathery caresses upon my lip scar and then my cheek. He further astounded me by uttering a word that sounded like 'shern.' I thought the German term meant nice or pretty and was surprised that he should perceive me as so. He withdrew his hand then and said gravely, 'Not leave me, Luthy.' The inference I drew from this was that I had the choice.

I was disturbed by this unexpected display of intense feeling and retreated into silence as I went about my chores. Josef's eyes, I frequently noticed, continued to observe me with hurt bewilderment, and I realised with a renewed fervour that I must attempt an escape very soon.

Cat stayed out that night, and I missed her. As I tried to settle on the now lumpy mattress, I became aware of an agitated movement at the farthest edge. I jumped up and quickly moved away from the bedding, terrified by thoughts of snakes. The sinking sun, reclaiming its light from the room, made it difficult to see the shadowed side of the mattress. My eyes never left the place. I bent forward to peer with a squint. Then out it sprang. A rat!

Panicking, it ran here and there in the dim light, around and across the room, and then it scuttled over my bare foot. A scream ripped from my throat. I was unsure where to run. We were in great fear of each other, that rat and I. Such was my panic that if the window had been set a little lower, I would have leapt out or climbed from it and then dropped.

Again the rat scuttled close, and my second scream resounded. I heard bounds on the stairs and the bolt rattling, and Josef was there. My abhorrence and terror of the rat were so great that I flew to him—to his rock-solid human safety.

'Ith a rat—a-a-rat!' I shrieked.

He turned and thumped down the stairs. Before I could follow, he appeared with a short length of timber. In horror, I watched as Josef hunted that rat, the explosive banging of the wood bringing violent barking from the dogs. And then the weapon hit home. He battered the rat again as it struggled to escape. After an awful squeal, it mercifully died—mercifully for all.

I had always held a sneaking pride in my courage in times of distress. However, bravery is not a quality to draw on ad infinitum; to me, this ordeal represented the worst of stresses. Indeed, if there was one thing that reduced me to a quivering mass of human cowardice, it was to be trapped with a rat.

I stood there shaking and sobbing uncontrollably. Josef dropped the piece of wood and came towards me. Without speaking, he took hold of my trembling hands for a brief, steadying moment, and instinctively I grasped his tightly. Then he walked over to the pulpy rat, picked it up by the tail, and flung it far out the window. His attention returned to me, still standing there whimpering and shaking, and I saw the light of genuine concern in his brown eyes.

'You good, Luthy?' he asked sympathetically.

I nodded. 'Yeth, I—I'm all right, Jothef.' I heard a tremor in my voice, a weakness I quickly tried to amend. 'It wath only a rat—but the *poor* little thing!'

After my shameful display over the terrified rodent, life began to seem more peaceful, and Josef became more … *solicitous*. No more did the door-bolt grate home at night, so Cat stayed out longer before delicately mounting the stairs to curl up on my mattress. I chose an evening when Josef seemed to be content and, in simple terms, asked if his parents had owned books. I was, of course, starving for literature.

Naturally, it had also occurred to me that there would be women's clothing somewhere, although from an older generation. My clothes were almost threadbare. To keep them clean, I alternated, wearing the green frock on wash days while the overalls and shirt discovered in the attic, dried on the line. Bloomers presented a difficulty, but I improvised and decided that any clothing would suffice until I could leave.

After a moment's deep contemplation, Josef responded to my enquiry. He stared—in an assessing manner, I thought—and then stood his height and went to the big bed. Kneeling, he withdrew from beneath it several boxes and a suitcase. It was like Christmas! His parents' clothes were there, and I saw books! I picked up the first but sighed in disappointment; it was of the German text, as were the next three.

So Josef was indeed German! It seemed a certainty then that he had never learnt to speak English. Nevertheless, I found several Australian comics and an old *Sydney Morning Herald*. I could have kissed that precious newspaper! He delighted in my pleasure and enthusiastically pulled out a longish frock and other articles of his mother's apparel. Then he handed me a sewing box.

'Oh, *thank* you, Jothef!' I was almost happy!

He smiled broadly, nodding at my unusual display of excitement. But then he ceased nodding, his expression grew serious, and his eyes clouded with anxiety. 'Now not leave, Luthy? *Your* bed now.' He gestured towards the high elevation of the mattress, blanket comfort, and blessed pillows.

My joy was brief. Alarm leapt in, warning that I had advanced from one dread to a worse! But I worried needlessly. He indicated merely that I alone would sleep there. To lend truth to this promise, he went up to the attic. I could hear him bumping around in there, and soon he dragged the rolled-up palliasse down the stairs. After moving the chairs away from the corner near the fireplace, he spread out the bedding and laid himself down to test the comfort of it. I thought he was taking a long time, but then his first snore came forth. I never slept in the attic again.

My sleep had been very sound in that comfortable bed, and in the morning, my first realisation that I was not in the attic came with a squint-eyed view of the board ceiling. Glancing around, I saw Josef bent over the fire and could smell the incense of burning eucalyptus leaves. Recalling the horror of the rat, I felt ashamed of my hysterical display over a creature no bigger than my foot.

When Josef saw that I had awoken, he strolled over to the end of the bed. 'Guten morgen,' he said gently, quietly, and then added, 'Sleep, ya?'

'Oh, yeth!' I exclaimed. 'And thank you tho much, Jothef!' I added as my sluggish thinking faculty clawed its way through the nebulae of sleep, and I willed him to read the earnestness in my eyes. He went to the table, and then, grinning behind his beard, he came forward with a mug of tea. I sat up against the pillow to receive it, smiling with gratitude. Immediately, he returned to the table. He smiled at me from across the room, and a couple of head nods conveyed, *This is very good!*—and a filmy veil began to slip almost imperceptibly over my intention to escape.

12

CAT

I couldn't help but regard Josef differently now, and I found attributes of kindness, self-sacrifice, and concern in his nature. This realisation supported my conviction that his keeping me a prisoner wasn't motivated by any degree of malice but by a natural need for the company of another human being. Age or gender was irrelevant—merely another creature of the same species as himself, for such was the extent of his loneliness. That, of course, posed the question: How long had Josef been alone, so absolutely, devastatingly alone?

One dewy morning, he stood hesitatingly at the door on his way to the meat house job and stared sidelong at me, then at the floor, and back at me. He seemed to be on the verge of speaking, his lips making preparatory movements. I watched, fascinated, as he concentrated. Then, quite suddenly, he turned to face me, lifted his shoulders, and pointed to his flannel-covered chest, and with careful deliberation, said: 'Ich bin Vierzig!' (My ears heard *F*earzig.) His grin seemed triumphant.

My surprise couldn't have been more profound, even though I had contemplated his earlier words, *Essen* and *Blut*. Some years ago, I had read about a German character in a library book and now thought that "vier" meant four. So I guessed that today could be Josef's fortieth birthday.

On that premise, I asked: 'You are forty? Then happy birthday, Jothef!' I wished even more than previously to own disciplined lips and tongue that would correctly pronounce his name. And then another puzzle presented itself: How did Josef manage to keep track of days and months? There was no calendar in the cottage. Perhaps in the shed? I inquisitively mused.

I worked hard that day, jabbing the spade into the impacted earth, tilling the ground for corn, beans, and other seeds recently discovered in old jars, hoping that some seeds would still be viable. With the prospect of 'normal' food teasing me, I thought of *Vegemite*, yearned for the taste and smell of a fragrantly ripe banana, drooled for a swig of wine—*any* wine—salivated for chocolate, and craved green vegetables, *familiar* green vegetables. I was beginning to hate dandelion greens, chickweed, wheat sprouts, nettles, and the other strange plants Josef gathered from the bush.

The sun was edging towards its zenith as I returned to the cottage to prepare lunch. My thoughts were focused on Josef and my desire to make the meal special, an optimistic attempt to mark this significant occasion of his mundane life. When he returned from his chores, I was bent over, stoking barely glowing embers.

'Cat dead,' he stated as prosaically as I might have said that the fire had gone out.

I dropped the poker and stared at him. 'How?' was all I could say, and I turned up my hands enquiringly.

'Schlange?' he answered, the querying tone and brief shrug conveying 'maybe?' He drew out a chair and seated himself at the table where I had placed his cold meat and 'exotic' salad. Yes, the culprit likely was a snake. I remembered seeing the slithering of shining jet scales retreating through the high grass near the hen run. I had been wondering that morning where Cat was, and I presumed she had gone hunting, a regular delight.

'Oh, Jothef! A thnake? Where?' I asked, his image suddenly blurring. He had already filled his mouth and raised an arm towards the yard beyond the door, which told me nothing more than I already knew, for she had not come in last night.

Now I was thoroughly stricken. To Josef, Cat was merely a mouse-hunter, but to me, she was a friend. I had grown very fond of that companionable little creature whose curled ginger body kept my feet warm at night, whose eyes followed my movements in the yard and watched over me as if I belonged to her. And it was Cat with whom I exercised my one-sided conversation, sometimes launching into quite long discourses on various subjects. I was anxious to remember my verbal skills, taught by the formal-speaking nuns and honed while working for *The Rivers Bend Weekly* newspaper.

Outside, I looked around and found Cat a few yards south of the pear tree, quite stiff; she had been trying to reach the cottage. Immediately I grabbed a spade and set about digging her grave, tearfully turning away Josef's offer to do it. I needed to expend my sudden excess of energy, and now I allowed convulsive sobs to gush unimpeded.

I wailed and dug, sobbed and shovelled, and when the hole was sufficiently deep, dropped to my knees and lined it with leaves from the pear tree. One last gentle caress of Cat's soft fur I bestowed, and then I placed her little body into the grave. With careful gentleness, I settled her as though she could still feel my hands supporting her, making her appear comfortable. I covered her with more leaves and then the brown earth.

I grieved deeply for that cat. Ironically, if anyone had told me my mother had died, I wouldn't have felt such raw emotion, for I had never known her. That aside, I was struck by Josef's apparent indifference. However, I acknowledged that he was desensitised to killing animals and occasionally finding them dead from various causes. It occurred to me then that until observing my reaction, Josef hadn't realised the extent of my devotion to Cat.

When I returned to the kitchen, Josef, now solemn and sad, handed me a small cross he had fashioned from sticks and string—his contribution to Cat's grave and salve for my feelings. Several times that day, I looked at the little cross and speculated on what religious instruction Josef had received when his parents were alive.

After placing his offering on Cat's grave, I sought flowers and looked across towards the slight incline below the shed, where I had noticed a few weeds in pretty bloom. On closer inspection, I found there were also some straggly survivors of a garden plot: rosemary, lemongrass, and parsley. I parted the tangled mesh of Kikuyu runners and found a forest of garlic, very much diminished in size. And there, shaded by a forty-four-gallon drum of water, was a healthy crop of mint.

Oh, the lifting of spirits I felt when discovering this herb garden! No doubt it had been Josef's mother's herb garden, for it contained plants for flavouring the otherwise bland food she cooked. Suddenly I longed to know everything about her and became frustrated, as often I had, over the lack of communication with Josef.

The swing from despair at Cat's passing to elation over the garden in such a short period was most taxing upon my emotions. I spent additional recovery time there, an hour according to the sun's position. Straightening my back, I left the garden to decorate the grave. Looking back, I fancied the herbs were smiling again, cleared now of the choking entanglement of grass and receiving sunlight. The little plot was my first garden since living at the convent, and I felt a peculiar sense of maternity. I found a new purpose there and resolved to nurture my plant babies tenderly.

Just on daybreak, my first thought was that something terrible happened yesterday. The realisation of Cat's death followed with a thump. I rose, wrapped a rug around my shoulders, and soft-stepped outdoors to visit Cat. I fell into weeping again when I saw what Josef had done. There upon the grave was a large, almond-shaped river stone with flowers carefully arranged on its smooth surface.

Presently, Josef emerged to stand beside me. 'Hund,' he said quietly, in explanation of the stone protection, and he patted one of the dogs curiously investigating Cat's grave.

13

LESSONS

Sometimes I wondered how Josef had managed to keep the farm thriving. His parents had taught him well. I deliberated on the value of the skins he traded: fox (primarily the highly prized white or albino), rabbit, possum, sheep, goat, and the occasional wallaby or kangaroo. The thought sidled across my mind then that there was likely to be a backup store of money left by his mother on which Josef could draw.

Common sense told me that in the past, the property was accessed by a vehicle-bearing road, now a mere track. On that road, Josef and his father would have brought in the materials (excluding bush poles and on-site mud bricks) for building the cottage and the shed. Perhaps they had a horse and a cart or sledge. How did the first generation of animals arrive? And why the excessively high fence? I asked myself for the hundredth time.

I knew that during the Great Depression, families took to the bush and built primitive temporary dwellings on government land. That aspect didn't surprise me regarding Josef's parents, for being German, they might have suffered at the hands and mouths of the xenophobes of the area. I pondered how many people were aware of the track and who knew that the family had settled here. So many questions to ask, and so frustrating to be denied the answers.

The intrigue generated by all this supposition occupied an increasing claim on my leisure-time thinking, and the quest for answers became more urgent. The call of the sea, the shack, and my belongings were always present, waxing and waning in strength and urgency. I had again determined to ask Josef to take me home. And yet—and yet now the realisation was growing that I would miss this big, gentle man who had given some form of meaning to my otherwise stagnant life.

My former instinct for ferreting out a story possessed me, and suddenly I longed for all my past writings and materials. Now I felt an urgent need to know Josef's story and wished to write about him, his parents, and this place in the middle of … *somewhere*. When had they arrived here? What had happened in Germany? I theorised. And how long would it be before he could tell his story?

Early each morning, Josef rolled up his mattress and stored it out of the way, and every evening he plumped it up and then spread it on the floor. One day while doing this, he encountered the opened seam through which I had accessed the raw fleece and discovered my coil of 'rope.' He held it up, his eyes widening, and looked at me questioningly.

Yes, I had blundered there—badly! I didn't imagine we would ever exchange beds. I should have retrieved the rope after he carried the mattress down from the attic, but complacency had set in. Now I had to think fast.

I remembered the convent's mat someone had fashioned by stitching coils of plaited rags together. I spoke the word 'mat' and coiled the rope on the floor to show how a mat, made thus, provides comfort. He seemed oblivious to the guile of this nervous explanation, and his face lit up with pleasure, perhaps recalling such a mat his parents had owned.

'Aah! Mat. Ya!' he exclaimed, nodding approvingly. I looped the wool over a chair, wondering what I had better do if I still wanted to leave this now cosy place—and big, trusting Josef.

That evening while lighting the candles and seeking diversion from my sorrowful thoughts of Cat, I recalled some German words gleaned from the library book. Water, I knew, was spelt W-a-s-s-e-r, so I poured a mugful and held it up. 'Wather!' I said with a lisp, hoping to impress him with my attempt to learn a few German words.

Josef grinned good-humouredly. '*V*asser,' he corrected, delightedly regarding me. I enunciated the corresponding Aussie-English and motioned him to repeat it. He said, 'Wor-tah.' It was hard not to giggle (certainly not derisively) at the child-like pronunciation, and I turned away to pat one of his worshipping shadows. 'Dog,' I said. He repeated the word and added 'hund.' Josef enjoyed the exercise, and I realised I had underestimated his intelligence. Perhaps living alone had slowed his mental faculties, and now, stimulated by company, his mind had awakened.

'Thith ith a table,' I announced, optimistically expanding a word to a statement, and awkwardly he responded—but with a lisp! I patted my over-baked mound of a damper. 'Thith ith *bread*.'

With pursed lips and brows raised, he swung his gaze from the damper to my expectant face and, after a considering 'hmmm,' took up the loaf and irreverently plonked it down. He shook his head. 'Nein! *Stein!*' Observing my vacuity (it was my turn to be stupid), he took his large self out into the twilight and found a stone. 'Stein,' he said, dropping it dramatically from a height to emphasise its solidity, and returned indoors, chuckling.

I was surprised to hear laughter emerge from my throat, and my appreciation for Josef's humour animated him to name objects around the room. I followed, pronouncing the English, and hoped we would soon share fragments of conversation, providing a better understanding and, eventually, answers to all my questions.

In the time that I had come to discover various merits of Josef's character, I noticed that he always became concerned whenever I even slightly hurt myself, checking the small burn or cut or graze often. In all this time, although he frequently inspected my head wound, he never referred to my badly-bruised thigh. The purple injury under my skirt was worse than the head wound, so his ignorance of it answered a question that had crossed my mind after regaining consciousness.

I learnt that there was an innate decency about Josef. I had noticed, on one occasion, that he even turned away from the mating procedure of the billy goat with one of the nannies and left them to it. There was nothing lewd about the man, and this set me at ease and earnt my respect. I warmed to him more.

Life at the little farm had changed from frightening to bearable and gradually more comfortable and interesting. Now it was quite pleasant. The sea still called me, but no longer was I desperate to escape, nor did I view Josef as a jailer. However, I had yet to test this theory by asking again when the long-awaited time came to sell more skins if I could accompany him.

After a busy morning, I rested at the table, missing Cat, but the new crop of kids gambolling about amid their mothers' stammering cautions filled the void with pleasure. I stirred the ambrosial pear-blossom honey into my tea. I had made cottage cheese that morning from the goats' milk. On my walk back carrying the bucket of milk, I noticed that the bean seeds, now serried loops of stems, were trying to pull their tiny-leafed heads out of the earth to receive the sunshine. Earlier, I had collected five eggs and discovered that one hen was broody. The pleasure drawn from the prospect of yellow, tweeting chickens now seemed hugely disproportionate to my plan to leave this place. On reflection, who would have thought I would be so contented?

Eric and Josef greatly contrasted. I knew that this man I was now living with would snap my husband in two if he so much as threatened me, and I cherished this conviction and the protected feeling it evoked. With that comforting thought, I gathered up my sewing and took it outside to the seat Josef had recently built. There, in the sun with my back against the warm mud-brick wall, I listened to the chortling magpies and watched Josef hoeing.

It was pleasant sitting there. My fingers worked hard to stitch another pair of bloomers cut from an old tablecloth belonging to Josef's mother. (It mattered little that the material's pattern was red-and-white check!) Feeling serene contentment in the spring sunshine, I reviewed my options. Did I still want to leave this place that I'd helped turn into a home? Indeed, I sought only simple happiness, the manifestation of complete freedom from the menace of oppression. And to what would I return after all this time? Someone had probably raided my shack to claim all that lay within its walls—my journals, my most precious possessions, no doubt destroyed.

Here I had a home, a solidly built *cottage*, quite an amelioration after the flimsy but much-loved shack that groaned and trembled with every salt-laden storm. Here I had a strong man to defend me. I reflected that Josef might be less intelligent than many, but what did that matter when weighed against his exceptional attributes?

I saw him bringing a bucket from the dam and watched his progress, noticing the manly squaring of his broad shoulders. When he drew closer, I saw that he was very pleased about something. He placed the bucket at my feet. Yabbies! Tonight we would have yabbies for dinner! Life was getting better all the time.

But one day, my newly complacent, almost Utopian world came crashing down. A stranger arrived. I watched as the movement of the human's approach disturbed the distant bushes and, as expected, saw it was a man.

'Jothef!' I hissed urgently, and he strode quickly over to the clothesline to see what had alarmed me. 'Thranger!' I said, peering around the washing and feeling much like an inbred idiot just crept down from the hills. 'A thranger!' I whispered again.

But it was not a stranger—it was Eric!

14

THE STRANGER

I could hardly believe it was Eric emerging from the scrub. I couldn't fathom why he sought me or how he'd found me. His approach was hesitant, and upon sighting Josef and the barking, lunging dogs, he stopped.

'I know Lucy's there,' he called out in an attempted bravado of voice and manner.

The washing provided a screen as I peered between the shirt and trousers. Josef stared at me enquiringly for a second and angrily flung out his arm towards the trespasser who dared use my name.

'*Who?*' he demanded and immediately glared back at the figure approaching the fence in small, tentative increments.

Now I stepped into the open. 'My—my huthband, Eric,' I told him.

Josef silenced the noisy dogs, and Eric slowly edged closer. 'I've been looking everywhere for you, Lucy. What the hell are you doing *here*—with *him*?'

My temper arose in a flash. 'What'th it to you, and why are you back? And how did you find me here?' I wanted to know everything at once. Josef glared at the intruder and looked wonderingly at me. Of course, he hadn't understood the conversation, only the words' sounds and the body language.

Eric appeared physically drained from his tramp along the rough track. He sat slowly on a stump and raised a soft-drink bottle to his mouth. His glances kept shifting quizzically, nervously, from Josef to me, doubtless aware that my bodyguard was in no way disposed to extend hospitality.

'Look ... the fact is Lucy, I—I want you to come back with me. I've got the chance of a good job now, but they prefer a couple, shearer and cook, and I thought we could get together again.'

I thought, *Typical insulting presumptuousness!*

But I said, 'Oh, *did* you? How very thilly of you! And what about *her*? What would your new woman think of that?'

'Well, the fact is,' repeated Eric, 'she went off with another bloke.'

'Well, *good!*' I gloried. 'Very gratifying to hear! Now you know the hurt of being two-timed.' I savoured my delicious moment and relished the thought of his nemesis. And all the while, Josef stood close to me and evil-eyed the intruder while remaining reserved and thoughtful.

Josef's silence seemed to imbue Eric with misjudged courage. 'Ah, come on, Lucy,' Eric said, 'don't be like that. You don't know the story.'

'Oh, don't I? All right then, *tell me.*'

'Well, to cut it short, she lost the baby, and—'

'The—the *baby?*' I knew my mouth hung open. I was utterly taken aback at that revelation, for I hadn't known there was a pregnancy involved in our triangular marital war. I tried to adopt a neutral expression.

'Are you the father?' I asked, attempting nonchalance.

He shrugged; the passage of time had rendered him indifferent. 'Who knows?'

'Well, didn't your girlfriend know who the father wath?'

'Huh! You're still naïve, Lucy! The fact is, with her, it was like—well, put it this way: if you sit on an ants' nest, you don't expect to know which one bit you!'

A-ha! The force of contrast had elevated me in Eric's estimation. He had learnt to appreciate the little virgin he'd enticed away from the convent. He had discovered the value of the blinkered loyalty and devotion it had been my folly to bestow upon him when I was young and dizzy with love for him. Well, I was neither now. But angry! Yes, *b-loody* angry! And bitterly jealous of the woman who had conceived so quickly and probably hadn't even wanted to.

Hey, God, that's not fair! screamed my un-lisping inner self at whatever constituted the power that manipulated the puppet strings of providence. In my heart, I knew I would have made a devoted mother. It was all I'd ever wanted.

It's not fair! I wanted to shriek at Eric, who knew it would unhinge me. However, for my own sake and to lessen his mean gratification, I held my tongue and managed to switch off those esteem-shredding thoughts of injustice to concentrate instead on the present drama.

I took a deep breath. 'Well, how did you find me?' I asked with feigned calmness, hoping to portray an air of indifference.

'The skin bloke—you know, the dealer—said that Ziegler had been buying a few luxuries lately; reckoned he must have a woman stashed away. He said I should investigate the couple of tracks that led west into the bush. I knew I'd picked the right one back there about an hour ago when I came to the old gate post with the sign on it.'

The word "Zeigler" sent a spasm of surprise through my inner self, but I suppressed all outward betrayal of it while my brain worked quickly to unite it with "Josef" and absorb the realisation that, contrary to my assumption, Josef's property didn't end at the fences.

'The thigh! Oh, how very clever of you!' I sneered. The sarcasm in my voice had reached new, almost enjoyable, altitudes. It was terrific how brave I was with big Josef beside me. Eric shook his head.

'Geez! It wasn't hard to find you, Lucy.' His sardonic tone carried a note of triumph, as though he presumed I'd been hiding, trembling in fear, thinking of him constantly. His almost cavalier air infuriated me afresh, but I withheld a further shot at him because his information, and the name Zeigler, intrigued me. Thus, I kept my hostile mouth clamped shut and listened.

All at once, there was so much to take in. Ziegler! *Ziegler*—Jewish? I looked at Josef with wondering eyes; he had indeed responded to that name. His imposing form approached the fence now. Eric finally drew on his limited reserve of wisdom and got to his feet, trying to appear unintimidated but stumbling in his haste nevertheless.

'You! Go!' shouted Josef, again flinging out his arm towards the track. The chain rattled as he began to unlock the gate.

'Righto-righto, I'll go, but Lucy's coming with me.' Even as Eric spoke, he knew it was an absurd statement. His feet continued steadily to increase the distance between himself and the leviathan opening the gate. He raised his voice and threw out a rapid string of words.

'Your stuff's still there, Lucy, all your books and writing things. We can start again. Job's waiting for both of us at the farm. You know the place—The Pines. I'll be waiting for you there.'

But an afterthought stopped him. He risked a moment's hesitation, and then he took a few paces forward, lowering his voice to announce: 'Lucy—geez, I nearly forgot to tell you! Sister Casima had a heart attack and wants to see you.'

To his credit, Eric nodded with a sympathetic gaze and observed me silently as I took that shock. Then he turned and retreated hurriedly into the bush. In retrospect, it surprised me that he had forgotten his trump card. To Eric, that news was expedient to his cause, a device to gain my compliance. But to me, it was a pure, immobilising shock. My legs weakened, and I sank to the ground.

In an instant, Josef was on one knee, asking, '*What*, Luthy? *What?*'

'Thithter Cathima, my—my *mama*, Jothef, ith very ill!' I said faintly.

A retrospective vision of her came instantly upon me. A sensation of quivering fullness rose in my throat, and I knew I was going to sob. Indeed, few among us have not cast aside that steely armour of maturity to submit for a moment to the influence of those primal elements—*mother* and *home*.

With leaden spirits, I knew that somehow, by some means, I would persuade Josef to let me make the journey, not only out of the bush to the road but to the distant town of Rivers Bend. There I would see again the woman who had always been the best of mothers to me.

For a while I was hardly able to recover my composure. In a preoccupied fashion, Josef and I worked through our chores that afternoon. He tended the animals, and I threw together a meal of basic fare, the simplicity of which hardly impinged upon my appetite, since I had none. That evening I sat staring at the fire for a long time, remembering Sister Casima. I glanced at Josef. His face appeared thoughtful and heavily clouded by a frown.

Presently, following a few minutes of pacing the floor, Josef sat near me at the table. He looked steadily into my eyes, took my hands, and pressed them comfortingly, and I returned the pressure. In truth, I became gratefully conscious of his manly proximity and, consequently, felt a stirring of sweet emotion. Then, after a silent moment, he amazed me by softly uttering in rich, deep tones: 'Schwester Casima—und Mutter Julia—und Schwester Maryann—und Fater Kline.' He enunciated the names carefully and with quiet reverence as he recalled them.

I was stunned speechless. A rapid flow of German poured from Josef then. Animated now, he stood and gestured with his arms. Struggling in his excitement to find the English equivalent, he struck his chest with firm resolution and announced: '*Ich teik*—*I* take, Luthy. *I*. To- t- t-morr– morgen.'

15

SISTER CASIMA

The time for *The Decision* was drawing near. Before the first shaft of sunlight speared through the window across Josef's mattress, he was up. Well before the dogs had scratched at the door for their meat, the rooster began his rasping command. Josef took the soap and a towel to bathe in the ice-cold water of the stream, and I soon had a bright fire radiating warmth and extra light into the candlelit kitchen. Dressed and back indoors, Josef vigorously towelled his beard and long, dark hair.

He paused suddenly in the flagellation and looked across at me, sawing away at another 'stein' for toast and sandwiches. Uttering a few German words, he used his fingers to imitate a scissor action close to the wild hair. At last! Now I would meet the person beneath the camouflage! I nodded eagerly and hurried to fetch the scissors from his mother's sewing basket before he could change his mind.

When Josef's hair lay thickly on the floor and he had shaved, I saw that he wasn't stunningly attractive (we were well-matched in that respect!). Nevertheless, he had an appealing, very masculine face, square-jawed with a broad forehead and, as I already knew, strong teeth. His eyes seemed more beautiful than I had previously noticed, and his chin had an indentation. Surveying the entire picture, it took only a moment to decide that I liked that manly face very much indeed.

I carried a basin of warm, soapy water up to the attic and bathed there, as had become my habit, rubbed my teeth with salt, and put on Mrs Ziegler's dark print dress, realising as it enshrouded me that she was a large woman. I appreciated that the dark material hadn't suffered accidents of rips, such as had befallen my old green dress. However, the skirt reached my ankles. Time was hastening, so I abandoned the effort to stitch up the hem and descended the stairs. Shortly afterwards, Josef and I emerged from the cottage looking antiquated but respectable in his parents' clothes.

We patted the bewildered dogs, shouldered our bundles, and Josef re-locked the gate. There was sufficient daylight now to see our way along the track, and, conscious of my hindering pace, I forced my feet to match Josef's strides as I followed. (It occurred to me that this spectacle might have appeared comical to an observer, had there been one.) We continued, facing hours of bush walking before reaching the public road.

After a while, we paused at the old gate posts to rest and drink water, and I saw fragments of the painted name 'Ziegler' still on the sign. As we strode along, I began to feel awed by the vastness of Josef's land behind us.

We tramped on, the rhythm of our strides awkwardly unsyncopated. The sun moved across the green canopy, and birds shrieked and twittered at our intrusion. Presently, the bush thinned to reveal tall spotted gums, each tree drawing its shadow around its feet, telling us it was noon. It felt a relief to rest on a smooth log while we enjoyed our egg-and-parsley sandwiches, simple fare and more delicious there in the bush after our prolonged, strenuous walking.

Fortified by food, water, and rest, we ventured in opposite directions into the thick bush for a moment's natural relief. Rested and refreshed, we swung into our old rhythm again, now with the sun on our backs. Kangaroos thudded away at our advance, and white cockatoos screeched and took to the midday sky.

Josef and I trekked on, and finally, through the trees, we glimpsed the biscuit-brown road. A quick thrill of excitement rippled through me, and he and I soon stood apart in blessed openness. Josef lifted his arm in answer to my enquiry, indicating that where he traded the skins lay farther in the southerly direction. But our destination was northward.

The town of Rivers Bend, where I had lived a semi-closeted life in the convent, was still a long way off, and already my feet ached. I longed to stretch my weary frame out flat, but we were racing the sun. An open-sided car slowed, but Josef, no doubt sensitively conscious of his limited English, waved the driver on. Later a truck and then a horse-and-cart came along, and he waved the drivers on as before.

So we kept walking. It seemed my pretended stoicism was working against me!

I kept my mind on Sister Casima. Apprehension mounted at the thought of her illness. I was nervous too of meeting again Father Kline and those good nuns who, quite naturally, had been so utterly opposed to my defiant alliance with Eric.

Josef answered my enquiries regarding his apparent connection with the nuns and the priest of St Declan's in German and English fragments. These teasing bits of information gradually coalesced to form a story of an occasional Mass attendance, the family travelling by a horse-drawn dray. I was probably an infant then. It appeared that afterwards they'd spent time with the nuns, who would have been grateful for the fresh eggs and cleanly dismembered rabbits. I knew them as kind women, the nuns; they would have prepared a healthful, filling lunch to sustain the Zieglers during the long journey back to the bush.

This information was intriguing! Already my writer's mind had mentally framed an opening paragraph! I resolved to glean more from Sister Casima, depending on the state of her health, or from elderly Father Kline, depending on the state of his memory.

Walking always helped me to think. As we strode along, my thoughts wandered back to the day Eric had left me, skipped over my blazing anger, and settled on the following week. That period had presented as the ideal time to look at my options, the turning point where I seriously considered returning to the convent to work as a maid if the nuns would support me. I didn't expect any payment but merely a home where I could continue my writing, the obsession which had begun years before with motherly Sister Casima.

My mind dwelt on her now. She was amazing. I could never adequately qualify my respect, admiration, and love for that good nun. The teacher of English and grammar at St Declan's had an intriguing story of her own to reveal. It involved a convict in her ancestry and a tale of scrawny children hungrily consuming a half-loaf of bread. At the same time, their anxious father watched from the door lest discovery should arise at the bakery.

I couldn't have had a better mentor, and I set about carefully recording her every word in exercise books. Later, with Sister's encouragement, I began an account of my formative years, and it grew into a depiction of restless adolescence evolving into an intimate chronicle of my romance with Eric. When I had last counted the journals, my handwriting had filled thirty-seven. Eventually, new pages of eager scrawl, which only I could decipher, moved into a different theme delineating the months as the cook's off-sider at Mr Bennet's farm where Eric was working, about a mile from Rivers Bend.

I reflected for a moment, recalling that in the early period of our marriage, we typified the quintessential happy couple. However, as passion burnt away and apathy fell coldly upon us, that idyll could no longer be applied to Eric and Lucy Chadwick.

As Josef and I passed by the eastward turn-off to the beach village, I caught the first fragrance of the salty sea and looked up at the sporadic drifts of seagulls sailing overhead. I became aware that a queer feeling of dread had dampened my excitement—Eric's connection to the place was the reason. I shook off the sensation, relieved that he was safely distant at The Pines. I was thankful there would be no confrontation when I turned beachward with Josef tomorrow on our return from the convent.

And nudging my mind now was the unsettling reminder that it would mark the final hour of my decision. Wandering recollections dwelt a moment at that critical juncture on the advent of my rescuer. And now, as if divining my thoughts, his voice brought me back to the present.

'You good, Luthy?' There he was, steadfastly striding beside me and not puffing as I was.

'Yeth, Jothef, I think tho. We'll be there pretty thoon.' He nodded pleasantly, so I presumed he had understood what my recalcitrant tongue was trying to convey.

The road led us uphill between pine plantations; then we walked through an Arcadian landscape of paddocks dotted with grazing cows. The sun hovered high over the northern horizon under a gentian sky, and king parrots of red-and-green plumage greeted us raucously as we approached the fringes of Rivers Bend. Wearily, our four tired legs mounted the last incline. We paused at the summit to admire the view of civilisation, and I felt thrilled to see the familiar configuration of the Town Hall, the spires of St Declan's church, and the row of poplars that bordered the school and convent. We both walked faster, and my heart swelled with sudden emotion when I saw Sister

Casima resting on the veranda, appearing as always in her black-and-white attire.

As he unlatched the gate, Josef waved to Father Kline in the garden, and the blessed nun looked up, exclaiming excitedly. She half-turned in her cane chair to call out to someone inside and then waved vigorously. In a moment, I was in Sister's arms, and copious feminine tears flowed, my past impious absconding-with-Eric forgiven, if not forgotten.

'Oh, my girl, how I've *missed* you!' her voice wobbled. I didn't dare speak, for mine was about to break. 'Missed your laughter, your chatter, and your-your *multitudinous* questions!' She laughed, heavily emphasising many words, as had always been her endearing way. 'And most of all, that *special* smile.' ('Special' was kind, flawed was fact.) 'I'm so *delighted* to see you again, Lulu.'

I felt the intense guilt of neglect stab my conscience and wished to have contacted Sister much sooner. I was embarrassed and ashamed that I had ignored her warning against associating with Eric. I had convinced myself that any tentative approach to the convent for reconciliation wouldn't be well-received. How wrong I was! How forgivingly and compassionately my foster mother accepted me!

The rich fragrance of baking bread wafted from the kitchen, and as Sister and I rested there under the wisteria-draped veranda, a smiling young girl with fair plaits looped up in ribbons appeared. She had brought us tea and Sister's favourite caraway seed cake, just as I used to do for visitors. After a few moments in the garden with white-haired, creaking Father

Kline, Josef ascended the steps. I was amazed at the affection in Sister's reception and the fond look of recognition in her eyes.

'Oh Josef, *Josef,* how *good* to see you again, dear! Oh, *look* at you! You certainly do evoke your father's image now. My goodness, where *has* the time gone? Oh, this is so—*so*—ooh!' she exclaimed, reaching for the large, outstretched hand.

I looked on with absolute pleasure at Josef's broad smile and friendly head nods, which, for the moment, rendered speech unnecessary. He seemed unaware of the extent of admiration accompanying Sister's superlative exclamations. However, he did manage a few concerned words of Lucy-taught English.

'You had bad, *bad* time Schwester Casima?' (How I wished I could pronounce Casima like Josef had!) 'Big pain like Mama?' he asked.

He patted a hand over his heart to clarify his meaning, and I saw that he understood Sister's answer in her formal speech, her head shakes, eyes to the sky, and then her reassuring smiles and nods.

'Oh, it *was,* yes, exceedingly painful, I assure you, Josef, yes indeed … but as you see, I have quite rallied. *Do* sit down, dears,' she said, a hand-flap indicating the double cane seat opposite.

I smiled self-consciously at Josef as we sat in our enforced proximity. It was a new experience, except for the day of the rat! I was hotly conscious of the massive build of him being so close, effectively dwarfing my frame. The transient sensation washed over me, a guilty feeling that we were like a pair of courting teenagers impatient for the blessed, veiling night to come, and

I smiled happily at Sister Casima. I felt duplicitous, though, as I noted her slightly prolonged, attentive gaze and wondered if her careful eye had detected a spark between Josef and me. I felt a warmth rush into my cheeks.

Once the preliminary greetings were over and the damp mother-daughter hankies pocketed, we focused on the anxious reason for the visit. Sister told us she was out of danger and expected to remain so if she kept a careful eye on her weight. Here she used her hyperbolic humour to declare that 'the weekly approach to the bathroom scales seems to cause the jolly thing to *tremble* most *fearfully!*'

Nevertheless, she admitted that the fright the heart attack had given her had enforced a new commitment to sensible eating. She joked about her old addiction to Mother Julia's cream sponges and lemon meringue pies. These delights were relative luxuries during the Depression, even though dripping had to be used in the pastry instead of butter. Her excitement over the visit engendered even a frivolous confession of midnight visits to the icebox treasure chest.

We had hardly noticed the dusk coming down when the whining mosquitoes sent us all indoors. There Sister Maryann was serving Mother Julia's cooking—delicious, uniting most agreeably with simple and sensible.

Jocular Father Kline made his smiling appearance afterwards. With an accent still hinting at his birthland many moons ago, he informed Josef of the room prepared for him in the presbytery. That sent my grateful thoughts to my old ornate iron-framed bed, with its cover of crocheted 'granny squares' waiting there in the convent.

Later that evening, alone with Sister Casima and savouring the almost-forgotten taste of cocoa and biscuits, I asked about Josef's parents.

'Oh Lulu, if you could speak German, Josef would tell you the entire account of it. He is—or was—quite an articulate talker in his own language, according to Father Kline.' She smiled at my surprised expression. When Sister Casima revealed this remarkable fact about Josef, I felt my heart swell. I immediately placed him on a tall pedestal in my mind and realised that I had better learn to speak German.

Sister made herself more comfortable and then began the story. Briefly, this is what I discovered:

Mr Ziegler was Jewish but had lived for many years in Germany. He had assimilated into German society and married a German woman. He was not of the orthodox tribe, so he harboured no qualms about attending Mass with his devoutly Catholic wife. But Germany was fast becoming a dangerous place for any person who was of even slight Jewish derivation. The story Josef's parents confided to Father Kline and Sister Casima was tragic.

Mr Ziegler, a farmer, had first become aware of trouble when he found one of his cows in the field near the road with a fatal stab to the neck. Further malice followed, and the family suffered increasing incidents of anti-Semitic inanities. Individuals wanting to impress their peers taunted Josef and his brother, Kurt, at every opportunity.

The Zieglers saw further discord gathering when their friends began to dissociate themselves from the family. Increasingly, Ziegler became aware that he would have to get his family out of Germany. However, his desire to leave as quickly as possible rendered him vulnerable to exploitation. He had no choice but to sell his farm for significantly less than its market value.

The menace of the frequent confrontations Josef and Kurt endured culminated when a gang of anti-Semitic youths attacked and bashed them as they attempted to cross a bridge. The teenage brothers were heaved together from the first section of the bridge where its approach rose from the bank. Josef entered a fathom of water and hit a submerged rock, leaving him with a severe head injury. However, Kurt missed the water altogether and met the dry rocks head-on.

The Zieglers believed it was murder. Officially, authorities termed it a 'fall.'

Josef slowly recovered from his head injury, but his parents soon realised that he seemed unable to speak and, therefore, couldn't immediately give his account of the attack. Mr and Mrs Ziegler knew the futility of chasing justice. Even had other eyes observed, no one would have dared come forward to support a young man named Ziegler.

Seeking safety for themselves and their surviving son, the Zieglers decided to migrate to Australia. Awaiting transportation, Mrs Zeigler gathered their marks, pfennigs, shekels, and her valuable inherited jewellery. With clever stitching, she concealed the gems in the shoulder pads, the hem, and the craftily-designed under-arm gussets of her overcoat.

The Zieglers' friends, the three Kline brothers—one of whom later became St Declan's priest—had preceded them to Australia. They were the first compatriot contacts in Sydney and provided much-valued comfort and assistance.

The plan for the Zieglers' future depended on the availability of a safe holding of secluded, bushed land with a creek and timber for fences and buildings. They had ample funds to pursue their new ambition. After a short stay in a Sydney boarding house, they bought a bushland property. Intending to use Mr Ziegler's farming knowledge, they took possession of the five hundred acres. There they began a new life, supporting themselves in a simple but resourceful manner, living off the land.

Sister Casima, yawning now and nodding to the girl waiting at the door to help her to bed, had one last surprise for me. She leant slightly to my ear and, with an air of having sanctioned whatever she surmised my alliance with Josef to be, half-whispered, 'Josef is an honourable person, Lulu. He's the excellent product of decent, hardworking parents; God bless them.' She patted my hand, as was her affectionate little custom, and nodded smilingly at me.

My brain felt as though it would burst with all the new information it had to process. I was amazed by what I'd learnt, and it afforded me greater insight into Josef's plight. I now felt a warm, maternal desire to protect him from further hurt. Sometime later, I smiled at the quixotic notion of puny me presuming to bestow protection upon that stalwart, gentle Hercules!

16

THE DECISION

The soporific qualities of the dinner and the warm bath afterwards blended with fatigue. Deep, restorative sleep came swiftly; I didn't even move from my flop-into-bed position. And yet somewhere in the creative and sensual recesses of my mind, a sweet dream had trembled into existence, and I floated in the ether of the delightful montage. The fleece of the old palliasse, washed and spun into skeins of soft, creamy-white yarn, appeared in my dream and rapidly transformed under Sister Casima's crocheting fingers into a bed rug for Josef and me. It was a beautiful dream, and I sought to hold on to it. However, the harder I tried, the faster it evaporated, until only wispy images of the lovely rug remained in my head to tease me.

When Josef arrived at the convent the following day, I was refreshed, ready, and waiting, although foot-sore and conscious of my calf muscles. It was pleasant under the oak tree, resting on the chain swing I knew so well.

I felt nostalgic, remembering my childhood, even more so because of my amusement over the current batch of convent pets, Sister Maryann's chief happiness. The pets afforded her a diversion from the daily expounding of the mysteries of arithmetic, geometry, algebra, and a little science. Indeed, her chief pleasure lay in caring for her birds and animals and nurturing the productive gardens. They were all industrious women, the nuns, and gave their time, ability, and love generously.

I don't belong to the sorority of sibyls and clairvoyants who flirt with the supernatural. *However,* amid this furry group of playful mischief was an adorable little female. The sole ginger kitten of the litter moved apart from her siblings as though transmitted by some other-world influence rather than of her own volition. She approached *only* me, as though drawn to me—or so it pleased my fancy.

Sister smiled as I fondled the warm little creature, and she hoped that all five of them would soon go to new homes. Impulsively, without the benefit of prudent forethought, I asked her to withhold the ginger kitten so that I might claim it sometime later. The promise imparted, she enquired with smiling curiosity, 'And what name will you give her, Lulu?'

She might have been surprised by the instant, nonchalant manner in which I distractedly phrased the answer. 'Her name's Cat,' I said, stroking the wriggling little thing, and Sister no doubt wondered why my tone suggested *of course!*

I relinquished 'Little Cat' and then took the parcel Sister was handing me. It contained a dress, she told me, and also something for Josef, but she requested that we defer the unwrapping until reaching the shack (for I had confided to my blessed foster mother the unsettling ambivalence of my impending decision).

We sadly farewelled, and I promised Sister Casima that I would return sometime soon—the convent was not remote from the shack if therein lay my independent and solitary future. Shortly afterwards, Josef and I left the arched gates, turned for a final wave, and began our walk to the beach. Pacing onward, I thought about the artful wistfulness Sister had applied to her comment that the convent needed an extra pair of hands now that she was 'forced into temporary idleness.'

I thought, *How happy Sister would be if I came home!*

I also thought of my old room, which had doubled as a sewing room after I'd abandoned it to marry Eric. The lace-curtained window overlooked the kitchen garden and the now emaciated scarecrow I had helped to make years before. I thought of the spongy softness of the rag mat as my feet stepped from the bed, the luxury of hot bath water, and the blessed convenience of the lavatory incorporated into the end of the back veranda.

Familiar to me was the faint waft from the gas stove and the kettle's cheery whistle, the herald of tea-making. Town living had many advantages, I reflected as Josef and I strode along the dusty road leaving the comfortable, civilised way of life behind.

The sun glowed directly overhead again as we turned our weary feet off the main road and began the walk that would end, at last, at the beach. Suddenly, there was the ocean! How beautiful it was! How it sparkled under a heat haze! We paused a moment to breathe the salty air. Presently, the first sight of the shack appeared over the dunes. It was leaning a little now—tired of waiting for me, I quaintly fancied. I felt a profound sense of *homecoming*, if one could apply that sacred term to my old abode, but the horrible, sullying memory of Eric wrecked the sensation.

And therein lay the decisive test. Would I be able to exorcise Eric's spirit? Would the ambience of all I had grown to love and idealise be present after my long absence? Would the call of the magnificent ocean anchor me there after all? Or would my fond attachment and increasing regard for Josef, my garden, his animals, and farm life in general eclipse even the convent's tempting comfort and convenience? At this point, my mind lingered for a wistful moment on the warm and fragrant bath water in which I had luxuriated that previous night.

Josef proved to be a gentleman. I knew he intended to accompany me at least to the shack, whatever my decision, and that he very much wished me to return with him to the farm. I was acutely aware of the depth of loneliness my decision may impose on him, made infinitely worse now for his having known the company of another person again. Josef had saved my life, and I was thankful, but I knew that if I went back to the farm with him, I wouldn't base my decision on gratitude but on wholehearted preference.

I was gripped by increased trepidation as we neared the shack, situated quite a distance from the scattered line of dwellings extending to the next defending arm of land that projected into the sea. My heart raced when I noticed that the door was slightly ajar. Perhaps someone was in there! But no, the dwelling was vacant. I hesitated a moment before entering. Josef stooped to come in yet still bumped his head against the door lintel. Silently, we looked around.

As expected, the contents had fallen prey to needy people struggling with only a few possessions. However, the building appeared undamaged. In a peculiar way, I appreciated the respect shown for the effort and resourcefulness that had gone into the shack's construction. The respect was accorded, perhaps unconsciously, by whoever had pilfered my small kerosene stove, kettle, teapot, hurricane lamp, striped horsehair mattress …

Gratefully, my eyes flew to my most valuable possessions—precious journals and money stowed in a hessian sack under the table and hidden beneath kindling meant for the outdoor fire Naturally, no one investigated that. Belatedly, a new thought occurred to me. If I returned to the farm with Josef—*if*, a small word used to convey so much meaning and with everything depending on it now. *If* I went back, he would have to carry the heavy bag for me—an imposition not previously considered.

Clear-eyed now, I looked about at the grim interior. It seemed so bare, dirty, abandoned, and unloved, and I had to suppress an immediate urge to tidy, to make it homely again. I sat at the rough table whereupon my pen had written so many words on many pages.

Josef, blocking the light from the doorway, glanced around disapprovingly. Indeed, how could he regard the shack otherwise?

His eyes seemed sad as they turned to me, sitting forlornly on the bare bed. His look conveyed disdain for the dwelling, and I understood it. With a clearer perception, I now saw the shack for what it was and wondered how I could have regarded it as 'home.' However, I conceded that its psychologically insular quality had represented the unique chance, free from Eric, to establish my independence.

Indeed, the fragrance of the ocean wafted over me now, that essence clinging to every surface, that zesty olfactory stimulant that encapsulates a multitude of feelings in all those who love the sea. For me, it still held a primal connection with the Ancients, with Homo sapiens when first discovering fishing, and with the down-to-earth wish to live simply. The grand rolling ocean with the towering headland to the north and the vast outlook of space beyond was soothing, and I remembered how this gift of creation had so often consoled me after Eric's abuse.

Nevertheless, once I had nullified my idealistic notions, I knew that all I now sought from this little dwelling was my bag of books. Moreover, I realised that my three-fold choices had changed to only *farm* or *convent*. I wished for sage guidance.

I had long since discarded my convent-instilled ideas about religion. Yet it had once been my pleasure to stroll along the hard-wet sand as the sun slid almost imperceptibly behind the birdcage shape of the mountain's peak and lose myself in beauteous nature. There I would talk aloud to the Great Unknown, hear what my ears sought to understand, and find blessed solace in that balm of imagined communion.

* * *

Josef's deep voice, richer for emotion, brought me back to the passing moment. 'I want, Luthy—*I want* you come back … the farm,' he said, nodding decisively, and with purposeful seriousness giving full emphasis to each word, he added, 'but *you* muth want.'

He moved to the doorway and looked entreatingly at me for a second before turning his back to stroll off down towards the water. I watched for a moment as his tall form entered the panorama of a deserted beach, peaceful under the noonday sun.

I gazed southward towards the ragged line of shacks and huts and didn't recognise any of the people near them, but my heart filled with sorrow when I saw that old Bill's tent was gone.

I sighed, sauntered indoors, and sat on what was left of the bed, feeling sad and almost lost in the emotional unrest of indecision. And then I remembered Sister Casima's gift. Eagerly, I withdrew the parcel from my bag and untied the string. I gasped when I saw the delicate, floral dress. Lilac was my favourite colour, as Sister well knew.

As I refolded the lovely dress, a white envelope slipped to the floor. I picked it up and walked down over the sand to where Josef stood gazing out at the horizon and silently handed it to him. As he opened the envelope, I glimpsed a photograph. Without turning to me, he strolled off a few paces, his head bent in studying the photo.

I saw his arms lift high. 'Vhy? Vhy?' he cried out to the vast, un-listening universe.

I was at his side instantly and saw that it was a snapshot of his parents and his much younger self taken outside the convent's arched gates. He dropped his arms heavily, as though the shock of his parents' image had depleted his energy, and turning to look at me, he held his hands outwards and implored again, 'Vhyfor, Luthy?' It was an anguished lament for past trauma, for Kurt, the injustice to his family, his years of solitary life, and the terrible, insuperable loneliness.

My heart lurched as I looked up at that punished face and those hurt, wet eyes. Without a nuance of reserve, I moved gladly into the outstretched, enfolding arms. I held Josef tightly, as he held me, as though I'd never let him go, and we both wept.

After a few moments of rocking and swaying there on the warm beach with gulls noisily rejoicing overhead and waves applauding, I drew back so we could look at each other's faces. It was then that I recognised with unequivocal certainty what I had been gradually learning all along—that this exceptional man was everything to me.

Gently, softly I said to him, 'They're gone, Jothef, gone,' and I added more positively, 'but you've got *me* ... we've got each other—forever.'

He looked down into my eyes, and this time it was the emotion that prevented him from speaking. But I didn't need to hear his words.

'Come on, Jothef,' I said. 'Let-th go home.'

EPILOGUE

I went back to visit the sea today, the beautiful, ever-changing, exciting sea, and found that it still surprised me! The children had never seen the ocean, and the visit was my way of celebrating their birthday. Josef ensured that our recently acquired ute had plenty of fuel in the tank and was ready to go. He didn't come with us, though, as he'd be busy all day salting down the meat from the steer he'd shot earlier and then preparing its hide for the skin dealer.

Naturally, Josef didn't want his beloved children to witness such a gory procedure, even though at age five they are already farm-wise, especially Kurt, who so much resembles his father and is named after his dead uncle. Shona is more like me and clings to gentler things, including Little Cat, the ginger kitten acquired years earlier from the convent.

Time's passing has eased Australia's economic hardship, and people have moved on to better living conditions. Nevertheless, a few weather-beaten dwellings are still standing, or leaning, on the sheltered side of the dunes, and the shack I once called home is now only a couple of posts covered in blackberry vines. As I sat on the warm dune watching my children play, I thought of Eric and wondered what he did with his life after our divorce.

Did I care, though? No, especially when I remembered his words, 'barren bitch.' As I waved to my darlings and enjoyed their laughter when their sandcastle tumbled down, I smiled at the superb irony of that mean taunt. Indeed, I had conceived shortly after Josef and I were married. So yes, there's victorious comfort there. But also there's satisfaction in the knowledge that Eric won't spread his damaged genes among the women he so eagerly associates with.

Shona looked back to see if I still watched them, and I sent her a wave. Although they're twins, my children are not alike, neither in appearance nor in nature. Kurt is larger and dark-haired, like Josef. He was born twenty-five minutes before Shona, so technically he is the elder. Like me, Shona is olive complexioned, with brown hair that will probably darken in a few years. Thankfully, both children are perfectly normal, so my nine-month fear that I had passed on a cleft palate was entirely unfounded. So I am the only lisping Zeigler in this little family.

Josef speaks English now, and I have learnt some German, but our children speak only English. Josef and I share the responsibility of their home-schooling; he has an astute mathematical mind, while I lean towards English, history, and geography.

The track Josef and I trudged all that time ago to visit Sister Casima at Rivers Bend is an all-weather road now, but it remains our private road. Sister Casima rallied after her heart attack and helped arrange our wedding at St Declan's. I still regard the dear nun as my mother, for it was she who brought me up. But lately I've been thinking of my birth mother, and the urge comes upon me to find her, especially now that she has at least two grandchildren.

But will she care? Is she even alive? Do I resemble her? Who was, or is, my father? I have no idea how to find the answers to my questions, and I doubt that I ever will. Still, there's a residual, fragile hope in my heart that one day a woman named Ida Ann Smith will seek me out. I expect that event would only occur via St Declan's convent, where she and I parted before my infant eyes could see her. I do wonder, of course, if Smith was her real surname.

I looked out at the headland, the waves crashing against the rocks and sending up sprays of white foam. I longed to stay, but we faced a long drive home, so I beckoned the twins.

By evening, the whimsical thought of finding my mother had grown somewhat stronger. That night after the children had fallen asleep, I lay beside Josef and watched the flickers of the dying fire dance on the ceiling. I was mindful of my unusual quietness that afternoon following our picnic at the beach and could have answered Josef's concern by referring to fatigue. However, there was more to it than that.

He propped his big self on an elbow, lifted a strand of hair back from my face, and looked into my eyes. 'Liebe, why so quiet you are today?' he asked gently.

I exhaled a long sigh and turned on my side to face him. 'It'th my mother, Jothef—my biological mother, I mean. Now and then I yearn to find her and know who my father wath.'

Josef kissed my forehead. 'Ya, ya, that is natural,' he replied. 'This, for the kinder?'

'I think tho. They don't know their grandmother.'

'Alive, your mother still is, maybe, Lucy?'

'Probably. Her age would be nearly fifty now.'

After a meditative pause, Josef said, 'So maybe put advertisement in the paper?'

'Yeth, that would be a good idea, darling—the *Herald*, you think?'

'Ya, good start that would be, miene liebe. Now—come here … mmmm.'

The next morning, I began to have a change of heart. After all, I reasoned, Ida Smith could have contacted the convent during my childhood to inquire if I'd been adopted, indeed, had I even survived. The nuns were the obvious link, and she never even tried.

But … well, perhaps something happened to her after she ran away from the convent, and she couldn't follow through for information about my welfare. I may never know. So why torture myself? What does it matter, after all? I am blessed with a fabulous husband and lovely children. Yes, a family of my own, so perhaps I should resist the inclination to resurrect the past, however tempting that challenge may be.

And yet I wonder, *Where is Ida Smith?* Perhaps Providence will bring us together one day, but will that be a happy reunion or a terrible mistake? Only God knows.

* * *

ABOUT THE AUTHOR

Born in Sydney, Catholic-raised and experienced in nursing, child-raising, and farming, Jennie Linnane expanded into freelance journalism and fiction writing, publishing articles and novels. She firmly believes that every person has a story to tell and enjoys helping others to write their memoirs.

"Behind the Barbed Wire Fence by Jennie Linnane is a compelling narrative that takes readers on a journey through the life of Lucy, a young Australian woman born in challenging circumstances and raised in a convent. Set against the backdrop of the Great Depression and the onset of World War II, this story delves into Lucy's tumultuous life, beginning with her marriage to Eric, which quickly takes a troubling turn."

- Joyce Nwaogazie, professional reviewer, editor, Goodreads

"There were twists and turns, surprise and drama … I was left guessing at what was going to happen next. My predictions were always wrong, though … it kept me on the edge of my seat." - Elvis Best, professional reviewer, OnlineBookClub.

"Lucy Smith … was left at birth by her young mother, entrusting her care to the Sisters at the Orphanage. Despite being born with a cleft palate and speaking with a lisp, Lucy's passion for writing, nurtured by Sister Casima, shines through."

- Lydia Efobi, professional reviewer, writer, editor

"I found this book interesting; the author's style of narration is commendable. She used a first-person narrative style, which made the book engaging and kept me glued to the pages. The diction is simple and portrays an intelligent articulation, making it easy to comprehend."

- Mercy M N, professional reviewer, editor and proofreader

www.ingramcontent.com/pod-product-compliance
Lightning Source LLC
LaVergne TN
LVHW011951070526
838202LV00054B/4888